KISS YOUR ASS
GOOD-BYE

KISS YOUR ASS GOOD-BYE

~

Charles Willeford

1987

First paperback edition
Published November 1988

Cover by Joe Servello

Dennis McMillan Publications
Missoula, Montana
Distributed by Creative Arts Book Co.
833 Bancroft Way
Berkeley, CA 94710

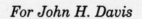
For John H. Davis

"Anything that doesn't kill you
will make you stronger."

—*Nietzsche*

1

I had been running around with Jannaire for almost six weeks before I found out that she was married. At ten p.m., Sunday night, when I started to leave my apartment house, planning to buy the early edition of the Monday morning *Miami Herald* at the 7/Eleven store a block away, I knew that her husband, Mr. Wright, meant to kill me.

Dade Towers, the apartment house where I live, covers a triangular block, and the building was constructed to fit all of the lot. Coming toward the building from LeJeune, it looks like the prow of a ship. If you approach it from College Drive it resembles a five-story office building. There is a main entrance on College Drive, with a Puerto Rican blue awning out front, and a telephone system and directory outside the locked door. To get the front door open you consult the posted directory, dial the apartment number, and if someone is at home and if he wants to let you in he pushes a button and a buzzer opens the door. When the door is opened, there is a large tiled patio-lobby, filled with glass and wrought-iron furniture. Beyond the

5

patio is a swimming pool surrounded by a wide grassy border. There are four Royal palm trees inside, and all of the ground-floor apartments on this inner courtyard have back entrances to the lawn and pool.

There is an elevator in the corridor to the left of the patio-lobby, and if you cross the open pool area to the other side of the building, there is another elevator. This second elevator serves the back entrance, and there is a tiled, lighted foyer here, as well, with a glass door leading out to Santana Lane. There is a streetlight just outside the doorway on Santana, and two steps down to the sidewalk. These steps are covered with green "no-slip" strippings. Across the street, on Santana, there is a large parking lot, but it is rarely used. Most of the residents nose into the curb around the building, parking on College and Santana. The Dade Towers parking lot across Santana Lane, which is required by Miami law, is used mostly by visiting guests, or by residents who have a boat on a trailer, or a camper to park—or in some instances, an extra car.

My apartment, 235, is directly above the back entrance foyer on Santana. I almost always park on Santana, and if the spaces are all gone, I park across the street in the lot. But I rarely park on College or enter the building by the front entrance. Whoever it was who shot at me knew that I would come out the back way, and they—or he—would know when I was leaving my apartment because the lights in my second floor apartment would be switched off. All of the residents in Dade Towers have an outside door key, and this key fits the front College Drive entrance, the back Santana entrance, and the two fire doors, as well. The locks haven't been changed in two years, and there are a lot of people in Miami who have keys who shouldn't have them. Laundry men, paperboys, ex-residents, aircon-ditioning companies, bug spray people, and who knows

6

how many residents have passed out extra keys to their lovers, male and female? Nevertheless, as apartment houses go in Miami, Dade Towers is safer than most, and the single women who live here like the security. The building, as I said, is two years old, and so far there has never been a robbery.

But because so many unauthorized keys are out, I was going to the 7/Eleven for a newspaper. I planned to crumple big balls of newspaper and scatter them around in my bedroom. That way, if Mr. Wright somehow got into the building, and then managed to get into my apartment when I was asleep, he would kick the wadded newspapers in my bedroom. They would whish or rattle into each other, and the sounds they made would wake me. I hadn't planned on what I would do after I was awakened, but the thought of being killed in my sleep, which was one of many possibilities, frightened me. I had been thinking about Mr. Wright's threat ever since five p.m. and by ten that night I was worried enough to take him at his word.

The single shot, fired from a moving, dark blue Wildcat, a car that roared out of the parking lot directly across the street as I stood on the steps of the Santana back entrance, missed my head by a good yard. But it was close enough to scatter a few bits of stucco from the wall, and some of these tiny chips stung my left cheek. The driver was making a right turn as he fired. He was driving with his left hand and firing across his body and out the window with his right. The Wildcat was moving about thirty miles per hour, and the car was about twenty-five yards or more away from me when he fired. The pistol sounded like a sonic boom in that quiet back street, and I figured by the sound that it was either a .45 or a .357 Magnum. With a gun that large, the marksman would have to be an expert to shoot accurately under such conditions, and the miss

7

of a full yard, for which I was thankful, was too close to be a warning shot. Whoever it was, and if it wasn't Mr. Wright it must have been a man he hired (or even a woman), had surely meant to kill me.

A split second after the shot was fired, which was already much too late, because by that time the car had reached LeJeune, I dived for the sidewalk, crawled into the gutter, and tried to wedge my two hundred pounds under a brown Datsun. I got my left leg and left arm under the car, but that was as far as I could go. As I lay there, struggling futilely to get all of me under the car, I could feel my heart thumping away, and my dry mouth seemed to be full of unwashed pennies. I am thirty-two, and I've been in a few barroom fights and in several situations where the danger potential was incredibly high, but this was the first time in my life that I have ever been afraid for my life. As this thought registered, I realized that I was in a vulnerable position. If the gunman circled the block and came back for another shot, here I was, all spread out for him. He could stop his car, aim straight down, taking his time, and . . . I scrambled to my feet and, running in a half-crouch, the way I had been taught in R.O.T.C. summer camp, I scuttled to the door, fumbled with my keys, and ran up the stairs to my apartment.

Once inside, I put the chain-lock on the door, and poured a double shot of St. James Scotch into a glass and added one ice cube. The quick jolt, which I downed in two medicinal gulps, helped so much I wanted to drink another. But I didn't. I needed a cool head, not a befuddled one, to think things out, to figure out what to do next. Mr. Wright was crazy, a psychopath. He had to be. Nobody, nowadays, shoots a man just because he thinks the man has fucked his wife. I hadn't touched Jannaire. I had intended to, of course, but that wasn't the same thing, and besides, I hadn't known that she was married. If I had known that

8

she was married, I would have made my plans accordingly. She was the most desirable woman I had ever met, and because I wanted her so badly, I had apparently overlooked the telltale signs of her marriage. She had fooled me from the beginning, and for no discernible reason.

The entire pattern was senseless and illogical, beginning with the electronic dating service, "Electro-Date."

2

Larry "Fuzz" Dolman, who also has an apartment in Dade Towers (319), is a friend of mine, and he became my friend—if not what you would call a close buddy—simply because we both happened to live in the same apartment house. We became friends through the accidental sharing of the apartment facilities. We used the swimming pool, and we played poker in the recreation room. We had both moved to Dade Towers when it opened, two years ago, and over this long period of time (two years is considered as a very long residency in a city of transients, like Miami), we had shared enough common experiences, together with Don Luchessi and Eddie Miller, to be more than just acquaintances.

Eddie and I were *close* friends, but Eddie had moved out of the building and was shacking up with a well-to-do widow in Miami Springs. We were still good friends, and we called each other on the phone two or three times a week, but Miami Springs is a long way from the South Miami area, and we rarely got together to do things any longer.

11

Don Luchessi, who had also lived in the building for a year, after leaving his wife, had finally gone back to her. Don still detested his wife, or said that he did, but she and the priest and her father and mother and brother had worked on him, and he finally made the sacrifice and was reconciled. He had an eight-year-old daughter he doted on, a spoiled, fat little girl named Marie, and he went back to his wife because of his daughter—not because he wanted to live with his wife again. No man in his right mind would want to live with Clara Luchessi. Clara would never stop talking, and all she ever talked about was her house and the things that were in it. She never left the house, either. She would never come with Don when he came over to visit Larry and me, and when we went to his house we had to listen to Clara talk about army worms, her glass drapes, a new rug-cleaning process she had discovered, and other domestic inanities.

And little fat Marie was also there, never more than six inches away from Don. When he was behind the bar mixing drinks, she was back there "helping" him. If he sat down, she sat on his lap. He had a pool table in his Florida room, but she spoiled the games we tried to play. She always wanted to play, too, and Don would let her. If she missed a shot, she cried and he had to comfort her. If she made one, she crowed. She also cheated, and Don let her get away with it.

Going to Don's house, which could have been a pleasant diversion, what with his heated swimming pool, his regulation pool table, and his well-stocked bar, was spoiled by his wife and daughter.

Clara was a great cook, one of the best cooks in the world, but even her wonderful dinners were ruined for you because she had to tell you exactly how each dish was made, and where the ingredients could be obtained. No one else could get in a word, or force her to change the subject. During Clara's vapid monologue, delivered rapidly in a shrill high-pitched voice, Marie made ugly faces, got down from the table from time to time to play terrible children's records on the stereo, and greedily finished her food as soon as possible so she could sit on Don's lap for the rest of the meal.

There is much to be said for the old-fashioned notion of having women serve the men first, and then eat their own meals at a second table in the kitchen.

For a full year, the four of us had had some good times together, but after Eddie and Don moved out, Larry and I spent more time together than we would have ordinarily. We went to movies together, rather than to go alone; we went out to dinner sometimes, rather than to go alone; and we sometimes went to the White Shark on Flagler Street to drink beer and play pool. We both loved to play pool, and as partners we were a deadly combination. We invariably won more games than we lost. But we didn't have much else in common. And the times were becoming more frequent when I preferred going to a movie, or out to eat somewhere alone, rather than taking Larry along.

Larry had a literal mind, and although I knew him well enough by now to know that he would and did take many things literally, it was a characteristic that one never gets used to completely. His interpretation of movies, for example, was maddening. He was unable to grasp an abstract conception. When we discussed *Last Tango in Paris,* he claimed that the reason Brando's wife had purchased identical dressing gowns for her husband and her lover was because she got them on sale. This absurd, practical interpretation of the identical dressing gowns makes Larry seem almost feminine in his reasoning, but there was nothing effeminate about him. He was tough, or as the Cubans in Miami say, *un hombre duro*—a hard man.

As an ex-cop, Larry had an excellent job at National Security, the nation-wide private investigation agency. He was a senior security officer, but not a field investigator, although he had a license, of course. He was an administrator, and worked in the Miami office on a regular forty-hour week. He never went out on investigative assignments. He has a B.A. in Police Science from the University of Florida, and his literal mind, apparently, was not a drawback insofar as his work was concerned. He wasn't allowed to say exactly what it was that he did at National Security, but his work had something to do with personnel assignments, and keeping track of cases and operators in the field. He made about twenty thousand a year, if not more.

Part of Larry's personality problem, although Larry was unaware of any problem, was his inability to taste anything. Something was awry with Larry's taste buds. He was unable to tell the difference between sweet and sour. Everything tasted just about the same to him. One night when we were both at Don's house, Larry took two bites out of a wax pear, picking the pear out of a bowl on the sideboard and biting into it without asking Clara if he could have it. The point is, he took the *second* bite before complaining that "this is the worst goddamned pear I ever ate."

The fruit looked realistic, all right, and anyone could have made the same mistake in the dim dining room, but no one with any taste at all would have taken the second bite. Larry would have gone on, in all probability, and eaten the entire pear if Don and I hadn't started to laugh. Clara, of course, didn't laugh. The wax fruit was quite expensive; she had purchased it from Neiman-Marcus' Bal Harbor store. On another night, he ate a colored soap ball in Don's bathroom. There was a full glass jar of these

14

pastel soap balls in there, and he thought he was eating a piece of candy. He didn't stop to consider that it would be peculiar to keep a jar of candy on a shelf beside the bathtub.

At any rate, Larry's lack of sensuous taste extended into tastelessness in other matters; in the clothes he wore, in his speech, and even in women. But there was nothing wrong with his olfactory organ. He had a keen sense of smell, which is unusual when something is wrong with your taste buds, and in a way, somewhat baffling when you consider that if he could smell the soap, and recognize the smell, why would he eat it under the impression that it was a piece of candy? All he could come up with in this instance was that "It smelled good enough to eat, so I thought it was candy."

When we went out together to eat, either for lunch or dinner, he invariably ordered a club sandwich. A club sandwich is easy to eat, of course, and it has all of the life-sustaining ingredients: turkey, ham, cheese, bacon (sometimes), lettuce, tomato, mayonnaise, three pieces of toast, and usually, pickle and potato chips on the side. At any rate, that was the reason Larry gave for always ordering a club sandwich.

I was sitting by the pool with a beer when Larry joined me, about five-thirty one evening. He told me that he had sent in a coupon and a check for ten dollars to "Electro-Date."

"What for?" I said. "There're about seven single women in Miami for every single man now. It's ridiculous to pay ten bucks for an electronic date. All you have to do is . . ."

"I know," he said. "I have a book with names and phone numbers, and if I got on the horn, I could have a woman join us here at this table in about ten minutes. But that isn't the idea."

Sitting there, with a secret widening grin, Larry was hard on my eyes. His silk shirt, stained with sweat, was yellow, and his Spanish leather tie was the color of dried blood. His textured hopsack jacket was orange, and his hair, Golden Bear styled, was haloed by the low sun with a 1930's rim-lighting effect. He took off his jacket, and draped it over a metal chair.

"All right, Hank," he said, "let's look at the evidence. If I made a phone call, and arranged for a simple date— dinner, a movie, and then back to my apartment for a couple of drinks and a piece of ass—how much would it cost me?"

I shrugged. "About fifty bucks. It depends on where you have dinner, and the number of pre- and postprandials you drink."

"Not necessarily. When you drive to Palm Beach every month, and you stop for a Coke and a hamburger, how much do you put down on your expense account?"

"Seven or eight bucks, something like that."

"Right. And you've made at least a three-fifty profit."

"About that, but on my expense account I'm entitled to a six-dollar lunch. If I take a hospital administrator to lunch, I can get away with a twenty-dollar tab, or, with drinks, even more."

"Exactly. So if I spend forty bucks on a simple date, and forty bucks is the irreducible minimum nowadays in Miami, and I can charge off the date to my expense account, wouldn't you say that I could get away with an over-all tab of fifty or sixty?"

"Sure. But a personal date, even with an electronic service, will be hard to slip by your office comptroller."

"You're right, Hank. Impossible, in fact. But not by the Internal Revenue Service. I can take the cost of the date off my income tax."

16

He took out his wallet, flipped it open, and displayed the photostat of his private investigator's license.

He said: "The idea came to me this morning when I saw the ad in the *Herald*. Instead of taking a chance on picking up a broad in a bar or a party who might turn out to be a drag, or a professional virgin, or a husband-seeker, I can get a date through the computer that fulfills most of my requirements in a woman. When I sent in the coupon and the check, I started a new file at the office. What I'm doing, you see, is investigating the possibility of using these women who sign up with Electro-Date as part-time operatives, to employ when we need them at National Security for special assignments. After each date, I'll fill in a mimeographed form I've devised on the girl, and put it into this new folder. I can then take the expenses of the date, padded, naturally, off my income tax."

"Did your boss authorize this?"

"The Colonel? Hell, no! He'd never okay anything this reasonable. This is my own idea, and I'll spend my own dough. But the point is, if I'm called down by the IRS, I'll have the folder with the info on the girls to show them. I *am* a private investigator, and one of my duties at National is to check background reports on possible employees. My reason for doing this, officially, is personal enterprise. I'm showing initiative, and if the Colonel ever finds out about my plan he'll have to back me up with IRS because he's a great advocate of personal initiative. Besides, it isn't costing National a dime."

"What's the real reason?"

"Compatibility. As I said, the girl who signs up for Electro-Date has to pay fifty bucks for five dates. The male client only pays ten bucks for his five dates. So much for Women's Lib, you see. But she will be favorably disposed to me from the beginning because she has put down on her form what kind of man she wants to date, or *thinks* she wants to date, which is the same thing. And on a first meeting, we won't need any elaborate setting, nor will I have to spend a lot of dough. We'll want to talk, to explore each other, discover our likes and dislikes. No movie, no Miami Beach first-date crap, with the big stage show and champagne cocktails. No. Just me. Honest Larry 'Fuzz' Dolman, and the sincere here's-what-I-think-what-do-you-think heavy rap. One hamburger, two cups of coffee, at Howard Johnson's, let's say, and I can take fifty bucks off my income tax for a so-called investigation. If I like the woman, and she likes me, on the second date I'll have her in the sack in my apartment.

"What do you think?"

"I don't know, Fuzz. In a way, it sounds almost brilliant. But it seems to me that women who would sign up for a computer date are either going to be dogs or desperate for a husband."

"That used to be true. The older dating services were mostly match-making matrimonial set-ups, but that isn't true any more. Women have changed . . ."

"When it comes to wanting marriage, women never change."

"The form will avoid such problems. All I have to do is put down that I want to date a woman who doesn't want to get married. A career woman, or something. Anyway, when I get the questionnaire, I want you to help me with it. You're the man with a degree in psychology, and these data forms have probably got a few catch questions."

"Why not?" I said. "We'll have some fun with it, and you can hardly go wrong on a ten-dollar investment. But if IRS ever calls you down, don't count on me to go down there with you."

However, you can go wrong on a ten-dollar investment, as Larry found out on his first date.

18

3

The questionnaire, when it arrived, was not what we expected it to be. What Larry thought, and was led to suspect, was that the form would be a series of multiple choice questions, all of them concerned with the personality traits and characteristics he wanted his ideal girl to have—like the tests they run occasionally in the women's magazines, with the things you like least versus the things you like best in a "mate." *Cosmopolitan* magazine has tests like these all the time, and any person with a fair grounding in psychology, and mine is a good one, can score a hundred every time on such tests.

I was particularly good on testing, anyway, because of my two years as station psychologist at the U.S. Army Pittsburgh Recruiting Station. It was my job then to weed out military misfits, to interview admitted homosexuals, actual and phoney, and to make decisions on whether to accept borderline enuresis cases or to send them home. The testing department was also under my supervision, although I had a Master Sergeant who ran this section for me. I was smart enough to let him alone and allow him to do things his own way, and as a consequence I learned a lot from him.

The only disagreement we ever had was about my attitude toward draftees who asked to see me because they were homosexuals, or claimed they were. Sometimes, oftentimes, they were not, and it was easy enough to tell when they were lying.

When you ask some innocent eighteen-year-old, "What do you do together, you and another man?" and he is unable to tell you because he has no idea of what two men do together, it is obvious that the prospective draftee is lying to avoid the draft. But I would reject him anyway, much to the annoyance of my NCOIC of Testing. The way I figured, if a man was so terrified of the Army that he would say that he was homosexual, even though he wasn't, he wouldn't make much of a soldier. And the first sergeants, down on the line somewhere, who would have to make a soldier out of him, had enough problems already.

But the questionnaire Larry received from Electro-Date had no questions whatsoever about his preferences in women. It was all about him—his age, his religion, his hobbies, and so on. This information would be transferred to a card, the card would be run through the computer, and then the cards that women had filled out—those that were similar in information to his—would drop out. He would be matched with one of them, and a date would be arranged between the two of them on the telephone by someone at the Electro-Date office.

"What you're going to have to do, Larry," I said, "is lie."

"Why?"

"Because the women who fill out their questionnaires are going to lie, that's why. For example, what's the upper age limit you'll agree to date?"

"Thirty, I suppose. I don't mind dating a woman my own age."

20

"There you are," I said. "If a woman's thirty-five, and she thinks she can get away with it, she'll put her age down as thirty. So you'd better put down that you're twenty-eight instead of thirty. You still might get an older woman, but at least you'll have some leeway.

"What's your religion?"

"None, really, but I used to go to the Unitarian Church once in awhile in Gainesville."

"You can't put that down. That's the last thing you want, a date with a Unitarian. They're weird, man."

"I know. They were weird in Gainesville, but they weren't inhibited, either."

"Put down Church of England."

"Episcopalian?"

"No. Church of England. That way they can match you with Episcopalians and lapsed Roman Catholics. If you happen, by chance, to get a real Church of Englander, they aren't concerned with morality, anyway. Episcopalians are all time-servers, and lapsed Catholics have a sense of guilt they're always trying to deny. A girl who thinks that sex is dirty, and feels guilty about it, can be a damned good piece of ass. If you were sincere about this questionnaire, I'd say put down Roman Catholic, because you'd probably get a lot of nubile Cuban girls. But they'll all be looking for a husband."

"How young?"

"Look at the newspapers. Usually, Cuban girls are married by the time they're sixteen. If they're nineteen and still single, they're desperate, Larry."

"Let's change Church of England then, and put down Roman Catholic."

"Why?"

"A desperate girl is ready for anything."

"You'll be flooded, Larry. Except for priests you're probably the only single thirty-year-old 'Catholic' in Miami who's eligible and unmarried."

"I like that. What about occupation?"

We had some fun with that one, but finally decided upon "Dietician." We figured that he would probably get a few nurses that way, or at least some healthy girl who was an organic food freak. We added an extra degree, making him an M.A., and provided him with some interesting hobbies: making models of World War I airplanes, collecting old bottles in the Keys, and spelunking for buried treasure.

Three days later Larry dropped by my apartment to have a drink, on his way to his first arranged date. We are about the same height, but he weighs twenty pounds more than I do. In his new white sharkskin suit, red silk shirt, with a white-on-white necktie, red socks, and white alligator-grained Ballys, he looked like a friendly giant.

"How do you like the suit?" he said. "Coat and trousers, four hundred bucks. If it wasn't for the expense account, I couldn't have afforded a suit like this."

"You're really pushing the IRS to the wall," I said.

"Not at all. The new suit comes under the allowance for uniforms, and a man has to dress for his job. If I have to date these women, in the pursuit of my investigations, I have to make myself attractive. Right?"

"What's the girl's name?"

He looked at a slip of paper, and grinned. "Shirley Weinstein."

I laughed. "That sounds like a nice Catholic girl."

"I don't give a damn," he said. "She might even be a Catholic, for all we know. A lot of people think my name is Jewish, you know. Dolman sounds Jewish, if you don't know any better. But no one would make that mistake with my old man, especially on St. Patrick's Day when he used to go around town wearing an orange tie and looking for trouble."

"Where does she live?"

"Miami Beach. Where else? In the Cresciente condominium on Belle Isle."

I whistled. "Those apartments start at a hundred thousand, and that's for a one-bedroom, with one-and-a-half baths. I've seen the ads."

"What's the easiest way to get there?"

"The Venetian Causeway is the quickest, I think. Another short one?"

"I'd better not. What are you doing tonight?"

"I thought I'd call Eddie. Maybe we can get together for some pool at the White Shark. If he can't get away, I'll probably take in a flick. But report in when you get back. I'd like to know how it goes."

I called Eddie, but he was flying to Chicago at eleven P.M. and couldn't drink. He said he'd call me when he got back. This was his last flight for the month, and then he would have at least three days off.

After hanging up, I found myself envying Larry. It was such a strange and formal way to meet a woman it was bound to be interesting. I didn't envy him the girl—Shirley Weinstein—I could pretty well imagine what she would be like, but the formality of the idea was attractive.

Women were not a problem for me. I could telephone two girls I knew in Hialeah, and if they were home, I could drive over and have a three-way orgy. There were a dozen names or more in my book, and half of these girls, if they had a date, would break it to go out with me if I called and asked them. Or, if I wanted some strange, I could cruise around and pick up a new broad within an hour or so.

But lately, it seemed, the women I screwed were all alike, as if they were cut from the same batch of cookie dough. The stewardae *were* alike, and practically interchangeable. Their apartments looked as if they were all

23

furnished by the same decorator. The clear plastic air-filled chair, the Budweiser bottle pillow, the *Rolling Stone* Mark Spitz poster (the one with Spitz lifting his trunks to reveal his pubic hair), the bottle of Taaka vodka, the tall stack of plastic glasses on the Kentone coffee table, the Port-au-Prince voodoo doll on the pillow, and the bed made up with garish Peter Max sheets—never with a bedspread—and the fresh uniform; always a clean, fresh uniform in a plasticene bag just back from the cleaners, hanging on a black wire hanger on the closet door; never inside the closet. Only the color of their eyes, hair and uniform was different. After a while, a few months back, while I was on my stewardess kick—with one leading me into another as I met the roommate, and she moved, and then I met *her* new roommate, who introduced me to her best friend, and then onto the next—they all blurred together.

They were even the same in bed, as if they had attended the same sex classes and had to pass an examination on *The Sensuous Woman, The Joy of Sex,* and the collected novels of John O'Hara.

Stewardesses never wanted to screw; with them it was all A.C.F.—annilingus, cunnilingus, and fellatio. You were lucky if one in ten would let you put it in. And there were more than 25,000 stewardesses living in Miami, all hot-eyed and eager to get a husband. They even smelled the same. Like milk. They usually wore musk oil, the scent that is supposed to bring out a true and personal odor, and that odor was milk; raw unpasteurized milk.

Nurses were a little better, but they had their peculiarities, too. At least one hand, but usually both hands, had to be touching you at all times; on the arm, the shoulder, the leg, and an arm was always around your waist when you walked. And a nurse's taste in civilian clothes was abominable. They looked great in their white

24

uniforms, brisk, clean, and iodoformy, but then they would put on a red dress or a purple pants suit, or a peasant blouse and a plaid skirt, and they looked as if they had closed their eyes and grabbed something out of a Goodwill clothing bin. But nurses were all right, much better than stewardae. They were earthy, dependable, predictable, and almost always on time.

The problem, of course, was me. Not the stewardesses, not the nurses, but me. I was bored with their conversational subjects, flying schedules and ports of call, hospital schedules and patients. I had been through the same conversations again and again, and I didn't want to listen to them any longer. But people always talk about their flying and floor schedules. I just didn't want to listen to them, that was all.

With Rita and Tina, the two Cuban girls in Hialeah, there was no talk at all. I didn't even know where they worked, or what they did for a living, although I had a hunch that they were divorcees on alimony. I would bring over a bottle of Scotch, undress as I fixed a drink, and then we went to it, all three of us, without any discussion. It didn't cost me anything, but a man has to be in the right mood for an orgy . . .

I left the apartment and went out to a John Wayne re-run, *The Train Robbers,* probably the worst Western the Duke ever made.

4

I had just finished watching the eleven o'clock news when Larry knocked on my door. He took off his jacket, refused a drink—he was already a little tight—and put a pot of water on to boil for instant coffee. He spooned two heaping teaspoonfuls of instant into a cup, and I asked him how it went.

"It was different," he said, after a long pause. "I've never had a date quite like it, and I had a much better time than I expected. It was weird, and gross, and yet I had a hellova good time."

He removed his tie and began to roll it around his finger the way I had taught him to do. I always do this, no matter how drunk I am when I get home. By rolling your tie into a tight roll, and putting it away in a drawer all rolled, it will be ready to use the next time without a wrinkle.

"This apartment," Larry said, "the Weinstein apartment, is on the top floor, the twelfth—not the penthouse, but the top floor. The Cresciente is on the bay side of Belle Isle, not on the ocean, but up this high, and on the southeast side of the building, with a screened veranda on both

27

corners, there's a beautiful view of the Miami skyline and the ocean, too.

"One hundred and fifty thousand hard ones, it cost."

"How do you know?"

"Irv told me. Mr. Weinstein. He was happy to tell me. He could hardly wait to tell me. Three bedrooms, three-and-a-half baths, a living room, a dining room, and a recreation room with a snooker table."

"A pool table . . ."

"No, a *snooker* table, regulation size, and two high pool room chairs, too. Irv had them made of rattan and fitted with custom cushions."

He stirred his coffee, and sat down across the coffee table from me.

I pointed the gadget at the TV set and switched it off. Larry said:

"The date didn't cost me a dime. I'd planned on taking Shirley to Wolfie's, or some place like that. I was a little nervous about this idea when I saw the Cresciente, but I was going to go through with it, anyway. But they had other plans. Mrs. Weinstein had fixed dinner, and on this first date they thought it would be best if we all just sat around and got acquainted with each other. Oh, yeah, they kept calling me 'Doctor.' "

"Did you go along?"

"Sure. Except I told them I was a Doctor of Philosophy. They didn't know the difference. I think the people down at Electro-Date must've told them I was a doctor. If it had been you, instead of me, you could've passed yourself off as an M.D. easy because you've got all that medical jargon down. But they were just as happy with a Ph.D. They figured I was a college professor, at first, but I told them I was working as a private investigator for National Security, and that I was planning to write a book later on the philosophy of security."

28

"What's that?"

"How do I know? You're always saying I can't think in abstract terms, but it went down okay with the Weinsteins."

"What about the girl?"

"I don't know about the girl. Shirley didn't say much. Her mother dominated the dinner conversation, and then I played snooker with Irv. So Shirley didn't get to say much of anything."

"Was she pretty?"

"It's hard to tell, really. These Jewish girls all look alike to me, you know, at least the ones on Miami Beach. She'd had a nose job but they took off too much, as they usually do. Somehow, that Irish *rétroussé* nose never quite fits a Jewish face. If you'd studied as many mug shots as I have the last few years you'd know what I mean. She had nice hair, though, black, long, and straight down her back—almost down to her ass. She wore round, lightly tinted blue glasses, and a full-length granny dress. She had a weight problem, I think—at least her face was chubby—but she was fighting it. She hardly ate anything at all during dinner."

"What did they feed you?"

"Whitefish, with the heads on and all, some kind of meat and tomatoes and cheese casserole, and a Caesar salad. I didn't eat any Whitefish. I don't like to see a fish with the eye staring up at you, and I was afraid of bones. Besides, by the time dinner was served, I was a little looped.

"Irv, you see, likes to drink, but I could tell he isn't allowed to have very many unless there's somebody else around. As soon as I'd drink half of my drink, and it was Chivas and soda, too, he'd say, 'Let me freshen that for you, Doctor,' and he'd whip over to the bar. He'd add a couple of jiggers to his glass, too, except that he was drinking a full drink every time, not a half-a-drink like me. The old lady noticed it, too, but she couldn't say anything to him with me there. Old Irv was really putting the stuff away."

Larry sipped his coffee, and said: "He's a retired furrier, about fifty-five, or -six, somewhere in there."

"What about the girl, Shirley?"

"Under thirty. I don't know how much under thirty, but she was definitely under thirty, and she was unhappy about the situation, the date. I knew she wanted to go out, to get away from her parents, but there wasn't any way to work it. And after dinner, once I started to play snooker, I didn't want to go out anyway. Irv is a good player, and he beat me the first game. But I beat him the second two games. His problem, he doesn't play enough with other people. He probably practices a lot, and you know how it is when you practice, you try a lot of shots you wouldn't consider seriously in competition because they're too risky. So he would try some of these risky shots, and he missed a lot. I haven't played any snooker for four or five years, and I didn't really get my eye back until the middle of the second game. I wish I'd known about the snooker table, I'd have taken my own cue stick along . . . "

I laughed. "Shirley would've appreciated that," I said. "Bringing your own cue stick along on a first date."

Larry laughed. "Yeah. But what I mean is the way it worked out."

"Did Shirley play, too?"

"No. She just sat in one of the high chairs and watched. She didn't say anything then, and before dinner and during dinner she didn't really get a chance to say anything. Her mother talked all the time, a real brittle woman, with a head of bleached blonde hair that looked like it was carved out of sandstone. You knew how hard it was just by looking at it."

"What did she talk about?"

"In a couple of weeks or so, all three of them are going on an around-the-world cruise. She talked about that. For the last year-and-a-half Shirley's been in Israel, living on a *kibbutz*. When they went to visit her there, Irv and Helen, they were so appalled by the living conditions they brought Shirley home. The water was alkaline, they had outside johns, the food was bad, the place was unsanitary, and they worked the shit out of poor Shirley. They had her running a buzz saw, making furniture. Shirley, I gathered, didn't want to come home, although she didn't say anything at the table. But this 'round-the-world trip is supposed to be a present to make up for it. That was the implication, anyway. Shirley hardly opened her mouth, but she looked at me a lot.

"Then, on purpose, but trying to pass it off, Helen, Mrs. Weinstein, said that the cruise would be a honeymoon gift for Shirley, if she wanted to take advantage of it."

"That was pretty blunt, Larry. Did they think, all this time, that you were Jewish?"

"I think so, yes. Irv didn't care, but Helen stiffened up when I finally said I was Catholic. And it upset Helen, too, when I said that I thought *they* were all Catholics and that that's what they'd told me at Electro-Date."

"They didn't tell you that at Electro-Date."

"I know, but that's what I said. Can you imagine some poor bastard getting married and having the mother- and father-in-law along in the same cabin for three months?"

"They'll find someone. He's got money, this guy."

"Irv's got money all right. He's rich, man. And a damned good snooker player. Why don't you and I go out for snooker some night? Did you ever play it?"

"I used to, but I don't even know where there's a table in Miami."

31

"We could play at Irv's. He said to call him any time I wanted to play. But that's out, I suppose. I'm not interested in the girl, and if I went back, it might give her a false idea."

"Did you get a chance to talk to her alone? You said she didn't talk much, but you haven't told me anything she said."

"Well, we didn't talk alone until I actually left. When I got ready to leave, her mother called her into the kitchen for a minute, and Irv went to get my coat. I'd taken it off when we played snooker, and left it in the rec room. When I opened the front door, Shirley said, 'I'll ride down to the lobby with you.'

"We got into the elevator, and about the sixth floor she pulled out the red emergency knob and stopped the elevator. I was still a little high, and when the elevator stopped suddenly that way I lurched against the wall. She looked into my eyes, through those blue-tinted glasses of hers, and said: 'Are you circumcised, Larry?'

" 'No.' I said.

" 'Let me see it,' she said.

"I took out my cock and showed it to her. She looked at it for a long time, as though she'd never seen a dong before, at least an uncircumcised dong, and then she said, 'I don't care.'

" 'What do you mean,' I said, 'you don't care?'

" 'I mean,' she said, 'that it doesn't matter to me whether you're circumcised or not.' "

"She was propositioning you, Larry. That is, she was telling you that she was available."

"I know that, Hank. I put it away, zipped up, and took the elevator off emergency. It really turned me off, man, not that I was turned on by her in the first place, but it was all so weird, standing there with half-a-buzz on, you know, with my dong out, and the way she stared at it. Maybe a soft, uncircumcised prick isn't a beautiful thing

32

to see, but it's mine, you know, and that curious, scientific look she had, the blue-tinted glasses, the way she leaned over, with her hands on her hips—I don't know, Hank, I just don't know. For a moment there, it scared me. I had a funny feeling, or a premonition, that it would never get hard again.

"Anyway, when we got down to the lobby, I gave her a good-night kiss, a long slobbery one. And she responded, too. But there was nothing there, man, nothing. My balls were ice cubes. So much for the first date. I think I'll put down about thirty-five bucks for this one on my expense account, and call it a night."

Larry rose, and picked up his white jacket. He put his rolled white tie into the left jacket pocket.

"Something's wrong with the computer at that electronic dating service," I said. "You couldn't have been matched any worse if you'd picked up a lez at a gay bar."

"I know. Tomorrow I'm going to call Electro-Date and raise holy hell. Even though I'm not a Catholic I said I was a Catholic and I'm entitled to either a Catholic or to someone who has lied about it the way I did."

I laughed. "Say that again."

Larry grinned. "I can't."

After Larry left, I thought about his strange evening for a few minutes, and then went to bed myself. The dating service didn't enter my thoughts again until I ran into Larry with his second date at Don's birthday party, a week later.

That's when I met Jannaire.

33

5

There were more than twenty cars parked on Don's lawn and along the curb and on neighboring lawns by the time I got to his house for his birthday party. The quiet of the suburban neighborhood was pothered by gibbering drums which pulsed above the shattering rise and fall of voices from the poolside patio. I learned later that some maniac had given Don a birthday present of three LPs of the authentic tribal drums of Africa.

Clara Luchessi, in a losing effort to keep as many people out of her house as possible, had centered the festivities around the pool and patio. The bar, the tables loaded with catered food, and even the two green-and-white striped tents, with extra swimming trunks and bikinis, one tent marked HE and the other SHE, as dressing rooms, were outside. There were no emergency latrine facilities at poolside, however. One still had to go inside the house to use the john, or else pee in the pool.

There was a lopsided pile of birthday presents on a card table at the far end of the pool. I added mine to the pile and checked the birthday card again to make certain the tape would keep it secure on the package. My present to Don was in poor taste, but it wasn't really for Don's benefit—it was for Clara's. I had found a used copy, almost in mint condition, of George Kelly's *Craig's Wife,* in Maggie's Old Book Shop, and I had talked Maggie into giftwrapping it for me. Don would read the play and laugh, knowing it was a joke. But if Clara read it, she might, quite possibly, take some of the pressure off Don around the house.

The soft night air was muggy, with the humidity at 90%, according to my car radio, but a warm heavy breeze huffed across the patio from the flat green fairway beyond the back of the house. Don's backyard pool was merely an easy lay away from the No. 8 green of the Miccosukee Country Club. Around the edges of the yard, and along the fairway border, Clara had placed lighted candles. They were upright in sandfilled paper sacks, and the surprisingly good light made the faces of the guests slightly distorted because they were lit from below. There was a strong electric light above the bar, however. The bartender, Joe T., or Jotey, as he was called, was a black man who bagged groceries regularly at the Kendall Kwik-Chek (sic). All four of us guys had hired Jotey as a bartender at one time or another for parties because he had surprisingly good judgment. If someone was about to get overloaded, Jotey would gently taper him off by reducing the alcoholic content of his drinks. Moreover, because Jotey didn't have to go to work at the Kwik-Chek (sic) until ten A.M., he would come back willingly, early the next morning following a party, and clean everything up for an extra ten bucks.

"Mr. Norton," Jotey said, as I reached the bar; "a J.B. and soda." He grinned, and handed me my drink.

"It's a lot better than Glen Plaid," I said.

Jotey winked, and waited on another customer, Nita Peralta, Don's chubby Cuban secretary. I admired her costume, a silk white-and-red awning striped mini-skirted dress, tied around her bulging middle with a red silk sash. She also wore strawberry mesh stockings and green patent leather boots. Not wanting to get into a conversation with Nita, I moved away from the bar.

I knew a few of the people slightly—Don's married friends—but most of the guests were middle-aged strangers. The older men, many of them accompanied by their wives, were Don's business customers, I supposed, invited to his birthday party so he could write it off legitimately as a business expense. Despite the heat, many of these older men wore dinner jackets and business suits. In Miami, the word "informal" on an invitation does not mean dinner jackets, it means sport shirts, Bermuda shorts, and tennis shoes or sandals. But older men, as a kind of compromise, almost always wear a suit and tie to "informal" parties. A suit for a businessman, like a soldier's uniform, is always correct, even though it's equally uncomfortable.

The weather in Miami is precisely the same as the weather in South Vietnam, and it's a damned shame that we cannot dress accordingly. When I call on doctors and visit hospitals, my company insists that I wear a suit and tie. I must keep my hair cut short, although the young doctors I see sometimes have bushy curls down to their shoulders. The rapport I gain with the older, far-right doctors, I lose with the younger far-left doctors.

I spotted Don right away. He was seated, with his daughter Marie on his lap, on the far side of the pool. He was talking to a middle-aged Cuban in a blue chalk-striped wool suit, and from the earnestness of their conversation, they were undoubtedly talking business. Don sold a lot of his English silverware to Cubans, he told me. His Cuban customers made up almost thirty percent of his business.

37

I decided to talk to Don later. Clara was at the other end of the patio, pushing the baked beans and potato salad. I wondered, maliciously, if she counted the red plastic spoons and forks after the guests left.

Eddie Miller had told me on the phone that he would be staying overnight in Chicago and would miss the party, so I searched for Larry. I ambled about, nodding pleasantly, but not stopping, to avoid talking to anyone. I knew that Larry would be there soon, because there could be no date cheaper than to take a woman to a free birthday party, and he said he would be coming with a new Electro-Date. After listening to his story about the Weinstein date, I was curious to see what the dating service would come up with next.

Movement helped a little, but the dull pain in my stomach was undiminished. I had gained five pounds, and when I gain five pounds I eat only one meal a day, at noon, until I have dropped back to 195. Eating once a day enables me to lose the necessary amount, and I can still have a few drinks besides. Ordinarily, I return to one meal a day as soon as I hit 200, but somehow I had crept up to 205 before I noticed it. As an additional psychological crutch to maintain my weight at a sturdy 195, I have all my clothes tailored. If I zoomed, suddenly, to 210, for example, I would need an entirely new wardrobe. And at that moment, at 205, my trousers were uncomfortably tight at the waist. I wore the tails of my sport shirt outside my pants to gain an extra eighth of an inch. It was all I could do to stay away from Clara's groaning buffet, but I was afraid to go near it.

I stood for a minute or so, nibbling on an ice cube and watching a wide-assed girl climb out of the pool across the water, and then returned to the bar for another drink.

I was on my third drink, and still hungry, when Larry arrived. He was wearing his white suit, his "dating uni-

38

form," and he moved like a snow-covered mountain through the crowd as he headed for the bar. The woman trailed him, and I didn't get a good look at her, even when he got to the bar, because she was on the other side of him. Larry put his birthday gift on the bar, a greasy, clumsily wrapped package in green tissue paper, and ordered two bourbons with Coke chasers. He was that way. He always ordered for himself and the woman he was with without asking what she wanted. With drinks, it didn't matter so much, but they corrected the order in a hurry when he ordered club sandwiches and they wanted a steak and a salad.

"What's that?" I said, tapping the package.

Larry grinned. "Don's birthday present. I got him a Colonel Sanders thrift-pack. Nine pieces of cold chicken. And I wrapped it myself."

"Your gift is worse than mine," I said. "I got him a book."

"Not really," Larry said. "I thought the thrift-pack might remind him of his batching days with us at the building."

"It will. But I don't think Clara will appreciate it."

"I hope not."

I picked up the greasy package, put it on the card table with the others, and returned. This time I got a good look at Larry's date. She was beautiful enough to know that the world would always be on her side.

Then I got a whiff of her, the full heady aroma, and it was like a hard right to the heart, a straight punch, with the entire weight of the body behind it. An odor, a smell, is almost indescribable, except, perhaps, in terms of other smells, but in one word Jannaire smelled Woman. I mentioned musk oil earlier, and the futile hope that it will bring out a person's individual odor. Most of the time it doesn't; it simply smells like musk oil on the user. It seems as if most of the women in Miami and half of the gay men use it, but this impression is false. If there are five women sitting together in a room, and if only one of them is wearing musk oil, it is so powerful that it blends with the perfumes the other four women are wearing, giving the surreptitious sniffer the impression that all five women are muskily anointed.

The musk smell on Jannaire was faint, because her own smell, or reek, to be more exact, of primeval swamp, dark guanoed caves, sea water in movement, armpit sweat, mangroves at low tide, Mayan sacrificial blood, Bartolin glands, Dial soap, mulberry leaves, jungle vegetation, saffron, kittens in a cardboard box, Y.W.C.A. volleyball courts, conch shells, Underground Atlanta, the Isle of Lesbos, and sheer joy—Patou's Joy—overpowered the musk oil. I was overwhelmed by the nasal assault, overcome by her female aroma, and although I could not, at the time, define the mixture—nor can I now, exactly—there wasn't the faintest trace of *milk*. Here was a woman.

"Jannaire," Larry said, "this is Hank Norton, my best friend. Hank. Jannaire."

She looked up at me with gold-flecked fecal-beige eyes. She was about five-two, but she looked shorter in gold flats. Her straight, dark brown hair, parted in the center and loose to her shoulders, was a dark bronze helmet, and it clung flat to her head as if she had just broken water after a shallow dive. There was at least a sixteenth of an inch of white showing beneath her pupils, and her bold dark eyes revealed the full optic circle. She wore a gold knee-length dress, shapeless at the waist and unbelted, with tiny golden chains for shoulder straps.

She raised her arm as Larry handed her the bourbon and Coke, and a thick tuft of black steelwool under her arm bugged out my eyes. Except in Swedish and British films, I had never seen a woman with unshaved armpits, and I mentally visualized the same thick inky hair of her

40

bush. Tiny stop and go rivulets of sweat inched down my sides as I began to perspire.

"Jannaire . . . ?" I said.

"She doesn't have a last name," Larry said. "She said," he added, in disapproval.

"How do you do, Jannaire?" I took the glass out of her hand, and placed it on the bar. "You don't have to drink that. You can have anything you want."

"I'd like a beer, I think." There was a catch in her voice, and she ended the sentence with a rising inflection. She ended all of her sentences with rising inflections, I soon discovered.

"I'll get you one," I said. There was no beer at the bar, but I knew there would be beer in Don's refrigerator.

"Stay here, Jannaire," Larry said. "I've got to make a phone call."

"We'll be right back," I said.

Larry and I entered the kitchen, and he jerked his head toward the hallway. "Let's go into Don's study for a minute."

We entered the study and Larry turned on the desk lamp. "Did you smell her, Hank?" he said. "Driving here from Hojo's in the car I had to turn off the airconditioner and roll the goddamned windows down."

"I'll take her off your hands, Larry," I volunteered casually.

"How? I can't just ditch her. She's liable to report me to Electro-Date, and I've got three more dates coming. Unfortunately," he said bitterly.

"No problem. You said you had to make a phone call. I'll just tell Jannaire for you that your boss sent you out on an emergency mission of some kind. You wait in here a couple of minutes, and I'll take her out to the golf course. That'll give you a chance to say 'Happy Birthday' to Don and bug out."

41

"You don't have to do this for me, Hank. I got into it, and I . . ."

"What the hell. You'd do the same for me."

"I'm not so sure that I would. What *is* that smell, Hank?"

"Woman, that's all, woman."

"Did you see her fucking armpits? I've never seen a woman with unshaved armpits before, have you?"

"No, but it kinda turns me on."

"It turns me off! After I finish the three other dates, I'm going back to stewardae. The hell with this income tax dodge. I keep running into one goddamned fantasy after another."

"Is Jannaire Catholic?"

"She must be. There isn't a Protestant woman in America who'd let hair grow under her arms."

"Okay, Larry. Give me a couple of minutes," I said, "and I'll get you out of it."

"Right. I'll just talk to Don a second, and split. It's a lousy party anyway, isn't it?"

"They always are."

I got two cans of beer out of the refrigerator, and rejoined Jannaire at the bar. Jotey, behind the bar, was pointing out Don and Clara to her with his long black forefinger.

"Let's go out by the golf course to drink these," I said. "If people see us with beers, they'll all want one."

I popped the tops and handed her a can as we walked toward the No. 8 green, and skirted the sand trap. The green was on a gentle rise of filled earth, and we sat on the grassy slope facing the lighted back yard. The row of candles along the border made the milling people around the pool resemble actors on a stage set, with the candles serving as footlights.

"Where's Larry?" she said.

"I don't know how to tell you this, Jannaire, but he said he simply couldn't stand you. So he left, and I promised to take you home."

"I could tell he didn't like me," she said, "but you don't have to take me home. I can get a cab back to the Hojo's on Dixie."

"Why Hojo's?"

"That's where I left my car."

"Larry's crazy," I said. "You're the most attractive woman here tonight. Perhaps you said something to irritate him. Larry's very sensitive, you know."

"I don't know what it could be. I know he didn't believe me when I told him I didn't have any last name, but it's true. I had my name changed legally to Jannaire five years ago."

"From what?"

"That's what he asked. But that's the way things always go with me. Men either like me or they don't from the first moment we meet. And more men dislike me than like me. It's always been that way, ever since high school."

"What do you do, Jannaire?"

"About men, do you mean?"

"No. I *like* you. We've already got that established. Work, I mean."

"Many of the women here tonight would know—a lot of them, I think. I design clothes, pant suits, mostly, under the trade name of Jannaire. I also own the Cutique, on Miracle Mile in the Gables."

"Cutique?"

"Awful, isn't it? But they remember the name, women do, and they come back. I also own two apartment houses, and I'm a silent partner in a few other business ventures. I keep busy."

"I don't understand this dating business, then. Why would a woman as attractive as you, and with some money besides—and a business—sign up with Electro-Date?"

43

She laughed. "Does Larry tell you everything?"

"No, but we're friends, and we live in the same building. And he did tell me about Electro-Date."

"To tell you the truth, Mr. Norton . . ."

"Hank, for Christ's sake. I'm not going to call you Miss Jannaire."

"All right, Hank. That's an odd name, too, isn't it?"

"Come on, back to the truth about the electronic dating."

"I happen to own twenty percent of Electro-Date, and it isn't doing very well now, although it started out well enough. Miami is much too small for accurate matching, which is always half-assed at best, but there're too many dating services competing. Anyway, when someone really bitches, as Larry did after his first date, they call me. I study the applicant's questionnaire and sometimes take the next date myself. I'm sure if Larry and I had had a chance to talk together, as you and I are doing now, I could've overcome his objections to me, whatever they are."

"No," I laughed. "Not unless you shaved under your arms."

"Fuck him, then! Do you want to blow a roach?" She opened her little gold mesh bag, and took out a stick.

"Go ahead," I reached for my lighter, "but I never smoke pot. It doesn't do anything for me, and I've been brainwashed. I'm a detail man, and by the time we've finished our indoctrination course, we never touch anything in the drug line."

"Mary Jane isn't a drug," she protested.

"I know the arguments. And I can counter every one you bring up, too. But in my job, with drugs of every kind available to me, I leave them strictly alone. They scared us so badly during training, I'm even nervous about taking an aspirin. And aspirin can be dangerous too. In some people, it burns holes through the stomach lining."

44

I lit her cigarette. She inhaled deeply, held it in, and said through closed teeth, "What's a detail man?"

"Drug pusher. I'm a pharmaceutical salesman for Lee Laboratories, and my territory includes Key West, Palm Beach, and all of Dade County. I'm supposed to see forty doctors a week and tell them about our products. I brief them, or *detail* one or more of our products, so they'll know how to use them."

"There're a lot of drug companies, aren't there?"

"Sure. And a lot of detail men, and a lot of doctors. But my job, especially for Lee Labs, is one of the best jobs in the world, if not the best. I work about five hours a week, when I work at all, and I make a decent living."

"How can you call on forty doctors in five hours?"

"You can't. I fake it, turning in my weekly report from the info in my files. Also I telephone from time to time—the doctors' secretaries—to make sure the doctor hasn't died on me since the last time I actually called on him. But I can usually make ten or fifteen personal calls in an afternoon when I want to. And if I set up a drugs display for one day in a hospital or medical building, that counts as forty calls for the week. I like my work, though, and I'm really a good salesman. I feel sorry for doctors, the poor overworked bastards, and I like to help them out."

"Do they always let you in? Just like that?"

"Most of them do. There are three kinds of doctors, you see. It's impossible for a doctor to read everything put out by the drug companies on every drug, but a few try. They all need a detail man to explain what a drug does, its contraindications, and so forth. So one doctor refuses to see detail men, and reads all of the literature, or tries to, himself. Another doctor never reads anything, but depends entirely on a detail man to brief him. The third kind doesn't read anything or see any detail men either. And if you happen to get this guy for a doctor, your chances for survival are pretty damned slim."

45

"So they see you, then?"

"Most of them, but you can't always overcome their prejudices or their ignorance. For example, I might ask a doctor, 'What do you know about migraine?' Half the time, he'll tell me that migraine headaches are psychosomatic, and that you can't do anything for them. He doesn't want to listen, you see. His mind is made up. In a case like that, you say, 'Okay,' and get onto something else. But when you're lucky, you'll run into an intelligent doctor, and he'll say, 'I don't know a damned thing about migraine. I get four or five cases a week, and I can't do anything for them.'

"So then you tell him. It so happens that we've got a product that reduces or even stops migraine headaches. What happens, you see, is that tension, or something, nobody knows what it is exactly, causes the blood vessels in your temples to constrict. Now this isn't migraine, not yet. But these veins can't stay constricted too long because you've got to get blood to your head. What happens, pressure builds, and the man can feel his migraine coming on. Then, all of a sudden, the tight veins open up and a big surge of blood gushes through these open vessels, and there's your migraine headache. What our product does is keep the veins closed. They open eventually, but gradually, slowly. Without the sudden surge of released blood, the headache is either minimized or it doesn't come."

"How did you learn all that?"

"Well, in this case, we had a two-day conference in Atlanta, with all of the detail men from Lee Labs in the Southeast present. We had a doctor who has spent his life studying migraine. He briefed us, and our own company research men who finally developed the drug briefed us. We had two films, and then some Q. and A. periods. Then we all got drunk, got laid, and flew back to our own territories. But the thing is, a doctor who came out of medical

46

school ten years ago, let's say, was told that you couldn't do anything about migraine. 'It's psychological,' they told him. So he still believes it, and he won't listen to you. And if he doesn't read anything, and he won't listen to you, if a patient has a migraine and goes to him, he'll tell him that the headache's all in the mind. It's a shame really, because such people can be helped by our drug."

"I've never had a migraine."

"They're pretty bad. They can last for hours, or even for days, sometimes. You're nauseated, and you lie flat on your back in a dark room with a wet towel over your eyes. It'll go away, eventually, but when a person gets a warning it's coming—you know, the tightening of the temples and so on—he has time to take our product and prevent the damned thing—or at least to reduce the force of it."

"Here," she said, passing me the stick, "take a drag. Sharing is part of the high, you know."

To please her, I took a short toke and returned the butt.

There was a happy shout, and I watched the guests gathering near the bar. It was time for Don to open his presents.

I rarely talked about my work, and not always truthfully when I did talk about it. But I had opened up to Jannaire, and probably bored the hell out of her. She had seemed interested, however, and the subject was interesting—at least to me. I wanted her to like me. She was a mature woman, at least thirty, I figured, and I couldn't talk to her about inconsequential matters the way I did with younger women. I also realized, sitting there, that I hadn't dated or slept with a woman older than twenty-five since I came to Miami. I wanted to kiss Jannaire. In fact, I wanted to rape her, right there on the No. 8 green, and yet I was reluctant to put my arm around her, afraid that I would be premature. Talking with Jannaire gave me an entirely different way of looking at a female.

47

"Do you want to watch Don open his presents?" I said.

"Not particularly. I should go, I think. I haven't even met the host or hostess . . ."

"This isn't a good time to meet them, either. Suppose we go somewhere and talk? To my apartment, perhaps?"

She laughed. "Apparently you like me better than Larry did."

"I'll just say 'so long' to Don, and wish him a happy birthday. Do you really want to meet him?"

"No, not in the middle of the big production number."

It was a production number. A circle of chattering bodies surrounded Don and the card table loaded with presents. Don sat in a chair beside the table, while his daughter, glorying in being the center of attention, opened the presents, one at a time, and handed them to him for inspection. Don would read the card aloud, and the guests laughed or applauded his loot. Clara, with a pencil between her teeth like a horse's bit, held a yellow legal pad. She would write the donor's name down, make a cryptic note of the present, and later on she would write nice letters of thanks, which Don would sign as his own. It was a grim business.

I stepped up to Don, put a hand on his shoulder. "Happy birthday, Don" I said in an undertone. "I'm splitting."

"What the hell is this?" He said unhappily. "Eddie is in Chicago, Larry just left, and now you—my best friends, for Christ's sake!"

I grinned. "Look what I'm leaving with—no, don't look now, and you'll understand."

I nodded politely to Clara, and ran after Jannaire, who was already at the end of the patio and opening the gate in the Cyclone fence that led to the street.

48

6

As I drove down Dixie Highway toward Hojo's I hugged the right lane and drove as slowly as I could get away with, wondering why I had exaggerated the healing properties of mygrote. Mygrote was effective in at least three cases in ten of migraine, but it sure as hell wasn't the cure-all I had claimed for it in my discourse to Jannaire. I never lied to doctors about the product, so why had I snowed Jannaire? I was trying to impress her, I decided, but I was going about it in the wrong way. Jannaire was more than just another cunt, and I would have to use other tactics to impress her, if that was what I wanted to do.

"Look," I said, clearing my throat as we stopped at a red light at Sunset Drive, "I've got two tickets to the Player's Theater tomorrow night. It's *The Homecoming,* a Pinter play. Perhaps you'd like to see it."

"Yes, I'd like very much to see it. But not if you're going to tell Larry Dolman."

"Tell him what?"

"That you're dating me, and that I have a partial interest in Electro-Date."

"Why not?"

"For one thing, he works for National Security, and I don't want those snoops to know anything about my business. For another, I've been lining up Larry's next date in my mind, and I don't want him to suspect that I had anything to do with it, you see. I have a hunch that he could be very nasty if he had a grudge."

"He could. I advise you not to play tricks on him."

"Oh, I won't." She laughed. "The trick'll be his problem, not mine."

"I don't tell Larry everything. But going to the play will just be the first date, Jannaire. My over-all plan, after I convince you how sweet and charming I am, is to get you into the sack. Eventually, anyway; I'm not going to rush it."

"A woman admires frankness, Hank, but you're awfully crude."

"Not crude," I laughed. "Basic."

I parked in the Hojo lot. She leaned toward me, kissed me on the lips, banging her wet hot hard tongue against my teeth. I felt the flames of her furnace breath for a second, and then she was out of the car before I realized what happened.

"I'll meet you at the theater," she said, waving, and climbed into her silver-gray Porsche. As she backed out of the slot, I noticed that the little car had battered front fenders.

† † †

There was no way, as I thought back on this first encounter, to tell that Jannaire was married. A married woman cannot easily get out of the house for two nights in a row. She had gone to Don's birthday party with Larry, and the next night she went to the play with me. Two nights later, I met her downtown at the Top of the Columbus for cocktails and dinner. The following week I had lunch with her twice, once at Marylou's Soul House, and once at LaVista. The lunches were both short, lasting less than an hour and a half each time, but she arrived on time, and left hurriedly because of business appointments.

My hours, the few hours I put in each week, were flexible, but Jannaire was always busy with her boutique (the Ugh! "Cutique"), her real estate interests, her designing, her clients, and with her home and husband. But I never, not once, suspected that she was married, or even that she had *ever* been married.

The evidence, however, or the clue, was always there, but I had failed, in my infatuation, my frustration—and there were times when her peculiar admixture of odors made me almost insane with desire—to recognize the obvious evidence.

She always met me somewhere, and she always drove home alone. I had never picked her up at her apartment, and I never had an opportunity to drive her home. With the number of separate dates we worked in during a period of almost six weeks—perhaps sixteen dates altogether—I should have suspected something.

The problem was, I was always trying to get her to come to my apartment. I had never concentrated on getting her alone at her place because she said that her aunt from Cleveland was visiting her for the season. She had established this house guest early, and I had accepted the aunt as a fact of coexistence. Also, from time to time, Jannaire would make an excuse to turn down a date because she was doing something or other with her aunt. That was another peculiar thing: why did she give me her home telephone number? I had no ready story prepared to explain to a jealous husband why I was calling his wife. I had no objections to running around with a married woman, of course, but to run around in Miami, visiting public places (I had even taken her to The Mutiny, the private club at Sailboat Bay) could have—in fact, it *did*— place a man's life in jeopardy. *My* life.

Except for the single, swift erotic kiss I got on parting— never on greeting—a kiss that always promised everything and delivered nothing, I was no closer to seducing Jannaire after six weeks than I had been on the first night at Don's house. I had cupped her breasts in the car a couple of times, as we were driving somewhere, and they were as firm as clenched fists. But that was all. When I propositioned her, which I did two or three times during each date, she merely smiled and changed the subject or smiled and continued to ask me questions about myself. As a consequence, Jannaire knew a great deal about me, but I knew very little about her.

I have never been in love. I'm not even sure that I know what love is, in fact, or whether I would recognize it if it ever happened to me. And I was not, in the sense that the term is used generally, in love with Jannaire. All I really wanted with Jannaire was to screw her and screw her and screw her, and that was all. But that "all" was getting to be an obsession.

It was Sunday morning.

Saturday night, Eddie Miller and I had gone to the White Shark to play pool and drink a few beers. The place was crowded, and it was hard to get the pool table. Once we got it, when our turn came to challenge the winners, we were able to hold it all right, but on our last game we played an old man and Sadie. Sadie, who owns the White Shark, also works the bar (the White Shark is a beer-and-wine bar only), and she had to keep leaving the game to serve customers, usually when it was her turn to shoot. The old man took a maddeningly long time to make his shots, and the single game of eight-ball we played with

52

Sadie and the old man lasted for almost an hour. Eddie decided to quit.

Two or three times during the evening, Eddie, preoccupied with something, had started to tell me what was troubling him, but each time he changed his mind.

I knew, or thought I knew, what was bothering him. He was still living with the wealthy widow in Miami Springs, a move he had made stubbornly against the advice of Larry, Don, and myself, and he had now discovered, I suspected, what a mistake he had made. The woman, who was still attractive, with a good, if rather lush, figure, was almost twice as old as Eddie, and she was undoubtedly smothering him. He wanted to talk about it, but was too embarrassed. I would not under any circumstances have pulled an "I told you so," and Eddie knew me well enough to know this, but he was still reluctant to talk about his problems. I didn't push him. He would eventually come around with his problem, whatever it was, and I would advise him as well as I could.

We left the White Shark at eleven P.M., Eddie to drive home (to the widow's house in Miami Springs), me to drive home alone to Dade Towers. He handed me a folded sheet of paper as we stood for a moment in the parking lot to suck in a little fresh, humid air.

"What's this?" I said.

"For now," Eddie said, "just put it in your pocket. D'you remember that game we played one night? The night you had us all make a list of everything we had in our wallets? Then you made a psychological analysis of each one of us from the lists . . ."

"Sure, I remember. But it wasn't fair as far as you and Larry were concerned. I knew you guys too well already. But I hit the girls pretty well, I thought."

"I thought so, too. I don't know how you did it, but that little chick I had, the Playboy bunny, turned as white as rice when you got into her about her father . . ."

"I can explain how I reached that conclusion. What she . . ."

"I don't want an explanation, Hank. We all laughed at the time, and you said yourself that it was inaccurate, at best, but I was impressed as hell. I never said so, Hank, but I was. I really was."

"It isn't a trick, Eddie. There is *some* validity to the analysis, but it's too general to be conclusive, for Christ's sake. On Larry's girl, the chubby brunette, I could say positively that she was a poor driver and she knew she was a lousy driver, because she had all of her earlier driver's licenses in her wallet. She had kept old ones, even when she got her new and current license. And she admitted, as I recall, that I was right. She felt, she said, that she really didn't deserve a driver's license, and it made her feel more secure to have as many as possible."

"That was sharp to spot that, though. I was impressed by that analysis."

"Hell, Eddie, you could've made the same comment. I was lucky on that one. She could've just had her current license, and I never would've figured out that she was, or thought she was, a lousy driver. Actually, she was a pretty good driver. She never had an accident, she said. If more people thought they were lousy drivers and drove more carefully, there'd be fewer accidents."

"I know, I know. That isn't the point. But what I've given you is a list of the shit Gladys carries in her handbag. In her wallet, and in her handbag, too. And as a favor—I hate to ask this, Hank—I'd like you to kind of look it over and give me an analysis of Gladys some time."

"Is there anything else you want to tell me about the problem, Ed? I mean, if there's something specific, I might be able to do a better job, even though it won't actually prove anything about what kind of woman she is."

54

"No, there's nothing specific I want to get into. I think I know what kind of woman she is anyway. Besides, I don't want to prejudice you any. I want you to be objective, as objective as you can, as if Gladys was a stranger, you know. I already know you don't like her . . ."

"I never said I didn't like her."

"I know you didn't. But I still want you to be objective." Eddie looked away from me, and took a rumpled Lucky Strike out of his beatup package. This was a sure sign that he was nervous. Eddie, to my envy, only smoked one package of Luckies a week. This single pack, by the end of the week, was usually wrinkled and battered because he carried it with him all the time. Sometimes he would go for two full days without even thinking about smoking a cigarette. I smoked two packs a day, and if I was drinking at night, I often went through a third. So when he did light a Lucky, it was easy to see he was agitated about his problem.

"That old trick of yours came back to me the other night, and I decided to try it," Eddie said. "On Gladys, but without her knowing anything about it. So this morning, when she took some clothes out to the washer in the utility room, I grabbed her purse and made this inventory—the one I gave you." He blushed, and took a deep drag on his Lucky. "I found out something about her already I didn't know. She's forty-seven, not forty-five. She lied to me, Hank. She told me she was only forty-five. But it was on her driver's license, her age, I mean, forty-seven."

I nodded. "She might be even older than that," I said. "She might've lied to the Highway Patrol, too. A woman who'll tell a black lie to her lover wouldn't hesitate to tell a white lie to the Highway Patrol."

"Jesus, Hank! Cut it out, will you? It's bad enough she's forty-seven without making her fifty, for Christ's sake!"

55

"I didn't say she was fifty. All I said was that she might've taken off a couple of more years on her license. The possibility is there, isn't it?"

"I asked you to be objective, Hank."

"I am being objective. That's what psychological analysis is, looking at every possible angle. There's nothing tricky about a wallet survey, Eddie. It just happens that we had this professor at Michigan, a Harry Stack Sullivanite, he was, who taught us how to look for shortcuts. We played this game in class with each other, and it was fun because it was so half-assed. The reason I got good at it was because I tried it again when I was staff psychologist at the Pittsburgh Recruiting Station. For example, if a draftee told me he was gay, and then I looked into his wallet and found a couple of condoms, a picture of his girl friend, and about five scraps of paper with girls' names and phone numbers on them, the evidence was contrary to what he said. It also worked the other way, with gays who claimed that they weren't gay, guys who wanted to get into the Army. I remember one gay sonofabitch . . ."

"Look, Hank, just go over the list for me, the one I gave you, and do what you can. It might be helpful to me. Okay?"

"I'll do it tomorrow."

"There's no hurry, man. Next week, the week after—I don't give a shit. Okay?"

"Sure, Eddie. I'll call you."

"I'm sorry, Hank. I got a lot on my mind these days. And that old man in there tonight drove me up the fucking wall."

"We should have gone to a flick. The White Shark's too crowded on a Saturday night."

"I couldn't have sat through a film. Goodnight, Hank."

So on Sunday morning, after I finished typing my sales reports and had them ready to mail out to Atlanta the

56

next morning, I pulled out the inventory Eddie had given me of Gladys Wilson's handbag. As I started to unfold it, a long yellow legal-sized sheet of paper, the phone rang.

It was Jannaire. The call was unexpected, because she had told me that she and her aunt were going to spend the weekend in Palm Beach.

"My aunt went to Palm Beach, Hank, but at the last minute yesterday afternoon I begged off. I tried to call you last night, but you didn't answer your phone."

"I went out to play pool, but I was home by eleven-thirty, baby."

"I called around nine, I think it was."

"You said you were going to Palm Beach, so . . ."

"I know. But I was lonely as hell last night. I wonder if you could come over for awhile this afternoon—around twelve-thirty or so, and I'll fix us a brunch. Did you have a breakfast, or are you still just eating one meal a day?"

"All I've had this morning was coffee. I'll be there at twelve-twenty-nine. What shall I bring?"

"Just yourself. Park in the street, not in the driveway. That's the arrangement I've got with my neighbors downstairs. They use the driveway one month, and I use it the next. And this month they're parking in the driveway. You've got my address?"

"Your address and your number."

"Push the bell twice so I'll know it's you."

My heart was beating a little faster when I racked the phone. At last, I thought, my patience has paid off. I refolded Eddie's list without looking at it, and threw it into the waste basket. Eddie's problems were probably unsolvable anyway.

I had about an hour and fifteen minutes to shave, shower, select the right clothes, and get ready for what I could envision as the greatest afternoon in the sack I had ever had.

7

Jannaire lived on LeJeune, in Coral Gables, in a two-story two-apartment duplex. Her apartment was the one on the top floor. There was hardly any yard in front of the duplex, and there were no garages. The neighbors below, whoever they were, had parked both of their cars in the short circular driveway.

I had forgotten, when she told me on the phone to park in the street, that there was no parking allowed on LeJeune in the Gables. LeJeune is the main four-lane artery that leads from Coral Gables to the airport, so parking is wisely prohibited. I drove around the corner and parked on Santa Monica. As I walked back I noticed that Jannaire's Porsche was also parked on Santa Monica, half-hidden by a huge pile of rotting vegetation that should have been collected weeks before.

I buzzed twice, and Jannaire pushed the buzzer from upstairs to open the door. The stairs, in the exact center of the duplex, were steep, and I wondered, as I climbed them, what this architectural horror did to the unhappy people living below, with the big wedge slanting through

59

the middle of their downstairs living room. Of course, architects do terrible things like that in Miami to build houses with additional space on small lots; but Jannaire, with the top apartment, certainly had the better deal of the two.

Jannaire was wearing a shorty nightgown and a floor-length flimsy peignoir, both sea-green. Her long brown hair was held in place with a silk sea-green headband. She didn't wear any make-up, not even the faint pinkish-white lipstick she usually wore during work hours, and her remarkable odor, which reminded me—perhaps because of the colors she wore—of the Seaquarium at mid-day, assailed and stung my nostrils like smelling salts. But instead of my eyes watering, my mouth watered, and I felt the firm stirring of an erection. The dark tangle of inky pubic hair was an irregular shadow clearly visible beneath the two thin thicknesses of gown and peignoir.

She kissed the air, not me, trailed two fingers lightly across my cheek, and told me to sit down. I sat on the long white couch, and gulped in a few quick mouthfuls of airconditioned air as she went into the kitchen to get the coffee.

The room was furnished uglily with oversized hotel-lobby-type furniture. There were two Magritte lithos on one lime wall, and an amateur watercolor of the Miami Beach skyline on another. A third wall, papered with silver wallpaper streaked with thin white stripes, held a blow-up photograph of Jannaire, taken when she was about nine or ten years old. The blow-up, about three by four feet, was framed with shiny chrome strips. In black and white, it held my interest, whereas the rest of the furnishings only indicated Jannaire's taste for impersonality. Everything else in the room, except for the blow-up photo and perhaps the two Magrittes, would have served as lobby furniture for any of the beach motels north of Bal Harbor.

There were even two lucite standing ashtray stands, holding small black metal bowls filled with sand. There were no books or magazines, and two droopy ferns, in brown pots, looked as though no one had talked to them in months.

I studied the blow-up photo, astonished that such a pudgy, unattractive child, squinting against the bright sun in her eyes (the shadow of the male photographer—probably her father—slanted across the foreground of the lawn) could turn into such a lovely woman. For a moment, the photo reminded me of Don's daughter, Marie, and I shuddered. I was immediately cheered, however, when I thought that there could be a similar future for Marie. Perhaps Marie, too, would be a beautiful woman some day; and for Don's sake, I hoped so.

Jannaire returned with the coffee, and set the silver service on the glass coffee table. I drank my coffee black, which I hated to do, and pointed to the blow-up.

"Whatever possessed you, Jannaire," I said, "to blow up that snapshot of yourself?"

"How do you know it's me? Do I look like that?"

"Not any more you don't, but it's you, isn't it?"

"No, it isn't me. It's my younger sister. She's dead now, and that was the only photograph of her that I had. She had others . . ." She shrugged, and twisted her lips in a rueful grimace ". . . but she burned most of her personal things before she killed herself."

"I'm sorry," I said. "It's always sad when a child commits suicide . . ."

"She wasn't a child when she died. She was twenty-two."

"That makes it even worse," I said.

Jannaire stared at me for a long moment with her glinting, sienna eyes, shook herself slightly, and said, "Yes, it does. Now, what would you like for brunch?"

61

"Do you have a menu?"

"No, but if you tell me what you want, I'll tell you what you can have."

"I'll have you, then."

"Scrambled eggs? Bacon? Ham?"

"No. Cottage cheese, with grapefruit segments, two four-minute eggs, fried eggplant, and an eight-ounce glass of V-8 juice."

"You don't much care what you eat, do you?"

"Not if I can't have you, I don't. And that's the truth when I'm only eating once a day. I'd rather eat things I don't like when I'm dieting this way, because I'm not tempted to eat any more of the same later on in the day. And I'll have a St. James and soda, too."

"I'll give you Chivas instead, and fried plantain instead of eggplant, but otherwise, you'll get the breakfast you ordered."

"Good! I hate plantain worse than eggplant, but it's just as filling."

That was the beginning of a strange afternoon.

I could not bring myself to believe that Jannaire did not want me to seduce her. I tried everything I could think of, but I got nowhere. After eating the bland, unappetizing breakfast, and I ate because she had either eaten already or said that she had, I had two more Scotches, switched over to beer when I began to feel them, and talked and talked. I grabbed her, I kissed her, and she got away from me. Once I chased her and got one hand between her thighs from behind, but she cleverly eluded me, fled to the back bedroom and locked the door. She stayed in there for almost an hour, while I drank two more beers, saying she wouldn't come out again unless I promised to let her alone. I promised, reluctantly, and she came out—this time fully dressed, wearing one of her slack suits.

62

I was sulky, pissed off and puzzled. There are ways to play the game, and there are certain unwritten rules to be followed. There are variations to the rules, which make the game interesting, but reliable patterns eventually emerge, one way or another, sets of clues, so to speak, and the game is either won or lost. I have won more games than I have lost because I have practiced the nuances and studied the angles a little closer than most men are willing to do. The discernible pattern, insofar as Jannaire was concerned, was the waiting game. By playing hard-to-get and yet by always holding out the musky carrot, I had recognized the classic pattern of her play early in our acquaintanceship.

She had called me for a date, or a meeting, almost as often as I had called her. She also, when we had met at a bar or a restaurant, paid her half of the tab, thereby establishing her independence. I didn't mind that. Tab-sharing, five years ago, was a rare phenomenon, but during the last couple of years it has happened as often as not—or at least an *offer* to pay half is made frequently. The insight required is to gauge whether the woman's offer is sincere, or merely a half-hearted gesture to indicate a show of independence. If it were the latter, and you guessed wrong, accepting the proferred cash, you could quickly lose the girl and the game. But there was no doubt with Jannaire. She would pick up the check, put on her reading glasses, total it silently, and hand me the correct amount of cash for what she had ordered. She didn't share tipping, of course, and in this respect I admired her perceptiveness. Women, when they tip at all, and most women truly hate to leave a tip, undertip—especially in Miami, if they are year-'round residents—whereas men like myself, who have a tendency, on other dates, to return to certain places, usually overtip. Overtipping is one of my faults, but I like to do it because I can afford to do so. By getting out of the tip altogether, Jannaire was able to establish her independence and essential femininity at the same time.

She was a mature woman and well aware of her body. Jannaire had admitted to twenty-nine, so I doubt that she was much more than thirty-one. She was beautiful enough to pick and choose. For every man she turned off by her earthy body odor and underarm hair, and she flaunted the latter by wearing sleeveless tops, and taking off her suit jacket in public places—as she had turned off Larry Dolman—she would turn on another man like me who was fascinated by the eccentric, the exotic, the unusual, the untried. Sergeant Weber, my NCOIC at the Pittsburgh Recruiting Station, had told me how sexy luxuriant growths of underarm hair had been to him in Italy during World War II, and to many other GI's, once they got over the initial shock. And it *was* sexy. Jannaire was a woman who wanted to know a man well as a person before going to the mat with him. She didn't have to fall in love with him, or even pretend to be in love with him, but she did have to like him; and the only way that she could tell whether she liked him or not was to get to know him fairly well. Once I had that figured out, I had set out deliberately to make her like me.

I thought I had succeeded. I had made my pitches at every opportunity, but I had made them lightly, and without using any hard sell techniques. Her rejections had never been outright turndowns; she merely changed the subject, or smiled without saying anything. It was the old waiting game, one I was familiar with, and a game I was willing to play.

After all, I had some other things going for me, and I could wait as long as she could, perhaps longer—unless she changed the pattern and decided she didn't like me after all—and she would be a more appreciated lay for

64

the delay. And if I lost, in the long run, there was a good deal of solace in the knowledge that the ratio of women to men in Miami, as I had reminded Larry, was still seven to one.

But here it was, Sunday, pay-off day, and the afternoon had been wasted. What was going on? The brunch invitation, the shorty nightgown, the exposed cleavage of hard, unhampered breasts across the table as I ate the tasteless food, the time and place available—and then, a runaround.

I sulked, sitting in a deep leather arm chair across from the white couch, and glared at her silently when she sat and faced me. She had combed her bronze hair, or brushed it, I supposed, and it was fuller as it touched her shoulders. Her alluring musky odor was fainter now, because of her jacket and slacks, and her freshly painted lips, playing card pink, almost matched the string of imitation pearls, as large as marbles, she wore around her neck.

I quit sulking, making an effort to salvage some dignity, buttoned my flowered bodyshirt, and yawned, stretching out my arms.

Jannaire, I concluded, was a lost cause. I didn't mind losing so much as I minded not knowing why. Although I wanted to leave, I was still curious about the why of the rejection. I was also feeling a trifle logy from the two Scotches and six cans of beer, and I had the beginnings of a headache.

She looked at her watch.

"Humphrey Bogart Theater will be on in a few minutes. D'you want to watch TV?"

I laughed. "What's the film?"

"Knock on any Door."

"He doesn't play Bogey in that one."

"We could play checkers."

"We've been playing that all afternoon."

65

"You can start sulking again if you want to. I think it's kinda cute the way you can pout with your upper lip without moving your bottom lip. How did you learn that, anyway?"

"By hanging around cock-teasers in the ninth grade. I thought I'd forgotten how but I remembered how to do it after chasing you around all afternoon. How did you learn such a good game of checkers?"

"What's the name of the film where Bogey has a plastic surgeon change his face, and then turns out to be Bogey when the bandages come off?"

"Did you ever read *The Chessmen of Mars,* by Edgar Rice Burroughs?"

"No, but I read *Tarzan at the Earth Score.*"

"You agglutinated that. When you were a kid you probably asked your mother for a napple."

"I did not."

"Why do you end every sentence with a rising inflection? 'I did not?' "

"Do I sound that way to you?"

"Not really. I can't get the little catch in the middle right."

"You're really angry with me, aren't you, Hank?"

"Not at this moment. I was for a while, but now I'm merely disappointed. Resigned, I suppose."

"I couldn't do it. I meant to, I intended to, and then I couldn't."

"Why?"

"I don't want to talk about it."

"Now I'm getting angry again."

"If you want to learn how to play checkers, why don't you study the game?"

"In other words, somewhere along the line in the last six weeks I made a wrong move, and that cost me the game?"

66

"Maybe I made the wrong move, Hank."

"I don't think so. Besides, nothing could make me mad enough to hit a woman."

"When you think, you frown, and when you frown your eyebrows meet in the middle."

"You've never met me in the middle. He escaped from San Quentin."

"And this girl in San Francisco took him in. He was trying to prove that he'd been railroaded into prison."

"Framed. You haven't eaten all day."

"I don't eat on Sundays. Sometimes, before I go to bed I . . ."

"And you don't screw on Sundays either. You watch Humphrey Bogart Theater."

"I have a toasted English muffin, and drink a glass of skim milk."

Downstairs, the door opened, and I listened as footfalls clumped up the stairs.

"Your aunt's back," I said.

"No," Jannaire said, "it isn't my aunt."

I got to my feet as she did. A man entered. He jangled some keys in his right hand a couple of times. Jannaire crossed to his side, put her right arm around his waist, and kissed him on the cheek.

"Mr. Norton," she said, smiling as she turned toward me, "this is my husband, Mr. Wright. And this is Mr. Norton, darling. Mr. Norton's in real estate, and he's been driving me around all afternoon showing me some properties. It was so hot in the car, I invited him up for a beer."

Mr. Wright, her husband, looked disinterestedly at the six empty beer cans clustered on the coffee table. He was in his early forties, and bald in front, but four inches of black side hair had been combed over the bald spot. He was about five-eight, slight, but wiry looking, and about 150 pounds. There was a deep dent in his slightly crooked blade of a nose, and the two deep lines in his thin cheeks were so well-defined they were black, as if they had been drawn with ink. He had a short upper lip, and to make it seem longer he wore a very long—practically a hairline—moustache. He would have been a plain, even an ugly, man, if he hadn't had such clear, penetrating, intelligent eyes. His eyes, bluish purple, with the black arching brows above them, almost made him handsome. There was a ragged pink patch of vitiligo on his forehead. His hands were huge, hands that belonged to a much larger man, and his thick wrists dangled below the too-short sleeves of his blue seersucker suit jacket.

"How do you do, sir?" I said. "I think the acreage west of Kendale Lakes is a good buy for your wife, and I'll be glad to show it to you sometime, Mr. Wright. At your convenience, of course." I looked at the beer cans, and shook my head. "Ha, ha, Mrs. Wright, I'll bet you'll think twice before asking me in for a beer again, won't you? But that sun out there really made me thirsty. Well . . ." I started toward the door ". . . you've got my phone number. It was nice to meet you, sir, and now I'd better get on home. My wife'll begin to wonder what happened to me."

"I'll walk you to your car," Mr. Wright said.

He followed me downstairs, right at my heels. I wanted to run, but I walked as casually as possible, matching his shorter pace as we shared the sidewalk.

"Were you showing my wife real estate all afternoon, Mr. Norton?" he said, twisting his head slightly to look up into my face.

"Yes, sir. All afternoon—since one o'clock."

"Whose car did you use?"

It was a trick question. But then, he knew her Porsche. Did he know mine?

"Mine," I said. "Why?"

He took a rotor out of his jacket pocket. "Because I have the rotor to my wife's Porsche."

We reached my car, and I took out my keys.

"Is this your car, Mr. Norton?"

I nodded.

"This car's been parked here all afternoon. I checked it four times, each time on the quarter hour."

I couldn't think of anything to say.

"You've been fucking my wife all afternoon."

"No . . . I . . ."

"We've already established that you're a liar, Norton. And your pants are unzipped."

I looked down to see, one of the most foolish things I've ever done in my life, and yet, it would have been impossible not to look down and check. My zipper was *not* down, but what could I say? My mind was benumbed. I fumbled with the keys, and finally got the door open. Mr. Wright stood in the open doorway, and held the door open as I slid in under the wheel.

"You cuckolded me in my own house, and in my own bed, Norton. And I'm going to kill you for it." His dark blue, almost purple eyes, stared at me coldly. He slammed the door, and stepped back.

I started the engine, and pulled away from the curb. Through the rearview mirror I could see Mr. Wright jotting something in a black notebook as he looked after my car. He was probably taking down my license number.

He is only trying to frighten me, I thought, and he has succeeded.

8

By midnight, two hours after Jannaire's husband had taken a shot at me, I had reviewed the steps leading up to it, and all I had to show for it was a hodgepodge of contradictions. They didn't hang together, none of them. I could discount Jannaire's lack of a wedding ring. Many married women nowadays don't wear one, feeling rightly or wrongly, that a wedding band is a stigma, a symbol that they are possessed by a man. So that didn't mean much, except, if she had worn one, I would have handled my seduction campaign differently from the beginning.

The aunt, I concluded, was certainly fictitious. On the other hand, when I had used the john in Jannaire's apartment, after the second, no, the third beer, I hadn't seen any evidence of male occupancy in the bathroom. So Mr. Wright—or Wright—I kept thinking of him as *Mister* Wright—was probably sleeping in the guest bedroom, or living elsewhere. She had said, "my husband," so they were still married, not divorced—or perhaps estranged. Estrangement, as the newspapers indicate every day, made him more dangerous than a husband who was safely and happily married and coming home every week with a paycheck. It was the estranged and jealous husbands who were always coming around to shoot their wives, their wives' lovers, and, if they had any, their children sitting in front of the TV set. If a lover was getting some, and they were not, it drove estranged husbands crazy. Almost every day when I picked up the paper I read about some jealous husband shooting up his house, his wife, or pouring sugar into the gas tank of his wife's lover's car.

That could account for Wright's mean-spirited attitude all right, and yet I couldn't be certain. The way he came in, juggling the house keys in his hand, the kiss Jannaire gave him on the cheek, and the calm way she greeted him—no anxiety showing, that I could recall—was almost as if she were expecting him. And if that were the case, although it seemed crazy to consider such a wild idea, she had set me up. She had set me up for the encounter, and she had planned, but had failed to carry through, to let me spend the afternoon in bed with her. Or so she had intimated—except that she couldn't go through with it.

If I could talk to Jannaire, or talk to Mr. Wright calmly and reasonably for a few minutes, I could straighten the entire matter out.

I called Jannaire's number, and she answered on the third ring.

"Jannaire," I said, "this is Hank. I . . ."

"Just a minute, Hank."

I waited, and a moment later Wright was on the phone. "Norton?"

"Oh," I said, "you're still there? Listen, Mr. Wright, I . . ."

"Where else would I be, Norton? You're a lucky man, and you've got a lot of guts calling here. But the next time I see you, your guts are going to be spread out on the pavement."

"Listen a minute . . ."

"You were lucky because the damned Wildcat I rented had this emission control that screwed up the engine. Just as I fired, the car surged and threw off my aim."

"They all do that, surge I mean. The emission control . . ."

"That's what the man at Five-A-Day Car Rental told me when I turned in the car. So I've got another car now, an older car, and next time you won't be so lucky."

"That's what I wanted to talk to you about. You're making a bad mistake, and . . ."

He slammed the phone down.

He was crazy, I decided, and so was Jannaire for living with him, or not living with him, whatever, or for ever marrying him in the first place. He was at least fifteen years older than Jannaire, and she was making plenty of money without him, so *why* had she ever married a nut like that?

I fixed a drink, a normal one-and-a-half ounce Scotch, with an equal amount of soda over ice, and noticed that my hands no longer trembled. I wasn't panicky, nor was I terrified. I was merely frightened, but it was a good kind of fear, the way you feel before a basketball game, or before making a speech on safety to a large group. In addition to my fear, and it was a fear I could control, I had an odd feeling of exhilaration, an emotion I hadn't had for several years. It was a feeling that came from thinking. Thinking was something I hadn't done for a long time. How rare it is nowadays to use your mind to think something out, to puzzle over something; and thinking about this idea, my sudden alertness and feeling of well-being startled me.

The sure knowledge, now, that Mr. Wright was going to shoot me, was a challenge and an insult. Did the crazy bastard think that I was going to let him kill me? Did he think I wouldn't fight back? I could feel the anger surge inside me—the way his car had surged when the emission control system grabbed it—and I choked it off. He wasn't angry. His voice had been cool, controlled, and without a trace of passion or anger. He was carrying out some stupid ritualistic code—the old unwritten law of the pre-Korean War years. A man fucks your wife, so you kill him to protect your honor. That was my lousy luck. Not only was I innocent—I hadn't even got so much as a finger in it—I had had the bad luck to run into a middle-aged husband with outmoded and outdated social values.

Wright would never talk with me. The rigid bastard was a damned reactionary, and, if he could, he would shoot me down in cold blood, dispassionately, feeling that he was doing the right thing and that he would be vindicated whether caught and found guilty, or found not guilty under the so-called unwritten law. The worst that could happen to him, the very worst, was a sentence of life imprisonment—if he were found guilty—and a life sentence meant that he would be released, at the maximum, within eight years. If he behaved himself in prison, and that is what reactionaries did—they always followed the rules—he would be released in about three years. For a crime of passion, a one-time killing purportedly done because of an emotional involvement, he could be out on the streets again—with a good lawyer and plea bargaining—within a year-and-a-half, or two years at the most.

If I knew this much, he certainly knew it, too, and there was now no doubt in my mind that he would try to kill me. And that is exactly what he would do, unless I killed him first.

So starting right this moment, Mr. Wright, I thought, I am going to be looking for you, and we shall see who will be the first one shot—you, or me.

I unlocked the front door, went to the trash chute down the hallway, and picked up a stack of discarded newspapers. After relocking my door and testing the chain, I crum-

74

pled up big balls of newspaper, scattered them on the floor, and went to bed. For a while, I lay on my back, watching the electric numbers flash on the ceiling from my electric clock projector, and I thought I wouldn't be able to sleep all night. But soon I got so sleepy I couldn't keep my eyes open . . .

9

I have always been a strong swimmer, but my forte has been endurance, not speed. And yet, here I was, flailing my arms in a loose Australian crawl, with minimum kicking, and I was ploughing through the water at three times my normal swimming speed. My head was high and out of the water, and most of my back was high out of the water as well.

The light was gray, misty, and swirling with patches of fog. I could only see about three or four feet ahead. A huge amorphous shape loomed in front of me, but I neither gained on it nor lost water. Whatever it was, we were apparently making the same speed. If I didn't know where I was going, or where I was, what was the hurry? I stopped swimming altogether. Strange. I didn't sink, and my steady pace continued. I sailed through the murky, pleasantly warm water, as if I were being towed. It was at this point that I felt the wide band around my middle. The band wasn't uncomfortably tight, but it was snug. I was tied somehow, and the band around my waist, attached to something or other (a submarine periscope?), was propelling me at top speed behind the shapeless gray form ahead.

The gray shape swerved sharply to the right, and a moment later I did, too, into absolute blackness. I wasn't frightened, although I was vaguely uneasy and more than a little puzzled. My pace didn't slacken as my chest parted the water. I clasped my hands, and rested my chin on my knuckles, peering ahead into nothing. Then, beyond the blacker shape ahead of me, the darkness began to lighten slightly, and I saw a half-circle of white in the distance. As the white circle became larger, I realized that I was in a tunnel, a curving tunnel, and a moment later I was bathed in hot pink light as I shot out of the blackness. The gray shape ahead of me metamorphosed immediately into a garishly painted wooden duck, much larger than me, and there were sudden splashes of dirty water between the duck's fanning tail and my head. I heard the sound of the shots then, craned my head and neck to the left, and saw the face and upper body of a man leaning across a wooden plank, perhaps a hundred yards away, aiming a rifle in my direction. For God's sake, I thought, as my arms flailed the water in an effort to increase my speed, he's shooting at me! I recognized, or thought I did, a patch of vitiligo on the man's forehead. *It's Mr. Wright, and he's shooting at me!*

† † †

I awoke then. The top black satin sheet was wrapped twice around my body, and the bed was soaked with perspiration. Thunder shook the skies, and torrents of rain sluiced down my bedroom windows. The electricity was off, which usually happens during these heavy Miami thunderstorms, and with it my airconditioning and clocks. It must have been at least 85 degrees in my apartment, although I didn't know at the moment how long the electricity had been off. My heart was still thumping in my chest from the nightmare as I disentangled myself from the sheet and staggered into the bathroom and took a shower.

Roasting in my bed, I thought, must have brought on the nightmare. Except that it wasn't a bad dream. Mr. Wright was real; he was looking for me with his gun, and I was indeed a captive duck in a shooting gallery—unless I did something about it—and soon.

At three A.M. the airconditioning kicked in. The lights were on again, so I fixed a cup of coffee. While the water was boiling I reset my electric clocks from my wristwatch. The power had been off for almost two hours.

In another three hours it would be light outside. The rain had slackened to a drizzle, and the coffee cheered me up some. I put an LP of "The Clash" on the stereo, and listened to them sing about the horrors of England, which were, if anything, much worse over there than they were in Miami. I started to cry, something I hadn't done in at least fifteen years.

Why in hell was I crying? Perhaps I cried because it was three in the morning, but most of all, I felt that I had lost something, something valuable and irreplaceable, even though I didn't know what it could be.

I added a jigger of brandy to my second cup of instant coffee, and stopped crying.

But I didn't go back to bed.

Somehow, the dream had frightened me more, much more, than Mr. Wright's promise to kill me.

10

The sun and my spirits rose but I was still tired and in need of sleep. I thought about taking a dexie or a bennie, or a half of one or the other now, and the second half at noon. One half of a dexie would wake me fully, give me a feeling of alertness, and provide me with the surge of mental energy I needed.

"I can handle it," I thought.

But these fatal words, flashing into my mind, changed it. This was the familiar rationalization we were all warned against during indoctrination, together with other grave dangers that specious learning and unlimited access to drugs faced detail men with in the field. Studying, as we did, the symptoms of diseases, the clinical properties of the drugs we touted to doctors—what they could and couldn't do—contraindications and side effects—the danger of self-prescription was always present. And because doctors as a group are not the sharpest body of men one will ever meet, especially if one ever talks to them about subjects other than their work, it is easy to fall into the trap of believing—of *knowing*—that you know as much, or even more, than doctors do.

Doctors work much too hard. They rarely have an opportunity to read anything, including newspapers. They are, as a whole, naïve politically, and unworldly concerning money, economics, or even interpersonal relationships. They make a lot of money, but they never have any because they invariably lose it through poor investments, and they spend it—or their families spend it—as if it came from a magic source. Many doctors, including those with the average $75,000 per annum incomes, who own two or three cars and carry a huge mortgage, have little or nothing in reserve. Bankruptcy is a frequent hazard for doctors, and they are then bewildered men, wondering where all the money went. There are exceptions, of course, but I had talked to hundreds of doctors in the last five years, and the overwhelming majority was poorly informed. They knew very little outside of their trade. It becomes easy, then, to fall into the trap and decide that you, who know so much more about the world than doctors, and have the same access to medical books, medical journals and drugs, can prescribe for yourself when you become sick instead of seeing a doctor.

The company had warned us about that, reminding us, at the same time, that the greatest number of drug addicts in the U.S., as an occupational group, were M.D.'s. Doctors, of course, used the same kind of reasoning that a detail man could fall heir to; they had practically unlimited access to drugs, and because they knew, or thought they knew, as much as any other doctor, they also had a tendency to prescribe drugs for themselves.

"I can handle it," they thought, and they would pop a bennie to get through a six A.M. operation, and then another bennie at ten A.M., to get through their hospital rounds, and then, because they were bone-tired, and beginning to get sleepy by one or two P.M., and they had an office full of waiting patients to get through, they would take a

82

couple of more bennies that afternoon. And so it would go, with emergency calls at night, and the first thing they knew they would be hooked—on bennies, or dexies, or nose candy, or eventually, if they had the right type of personality (and many did), on morphine or one of its more readily available derivatives.

When you get sick, the company told us, see a doctor. Never, never take a self-prescribed drug of any kind. The rule was a good one, because no one can handle it. No one.

With a shrug, I skipped the bennie, and settled for a close shave and a long cold shower. I put on a pair of gray seersucker slacks and a sportshirt, brewed fresh coffee, and sat down to decide my next move.

Luckily, my reports were made out and ready to mail to Atlanta. It wasn't essential to call on any doctors during the week. I could fake another set of calls on the following Saturday or Sunday when I made my next report, and it made no difference. The sales in my territory were the highest in the Southeastern District. I could devote full time to protecting myself, or better, I could reverse the rôle. I could hunt down Mr. Wright, and put *him* on the defensive. I didn't want to shoot him, or hurt him in any way, but I had to get him alone somewhere and talk to him. I was positive, if I could only talk to him for a while, and explain how Jannaire had passed herself off as a single, unattached woman, and that there had never been anything physical between us, he would see how foolish it was to come after me with a gun.

Jannaire, in all probability, had told him the same thing by now—that there had been no sex between us—and maybe he had cooled off already, during the night. On the other hand, he might not believe Jannaire. She might have had, for all I knew, a long record of clandestine lovers, and if so, Mr. Wright would discount anything she said.

83

I had to get a gun. What was the best way to go about getting one, and obtaining a license to carry it? Larry Dolman would know, but so would Alton Thead. I couldn't go to Larry. I didn't want Larry to find out about my predicament. He would help me, of course, but if he did, the nature of our relationship would be altered. He believed that I was screwing Jannaire. Without actually saying so, I had implied as much a few days before when I ran into him at the mailboxes in the lobby. If Larry knew that I had been running around with her for six weeks without getting any, and without even learning that she was married, he would be contemptuous. It was bad enough to be contemptuous of myself, but I couldn't stand it from Larry. In his opinion, and in Don's and Eddie's as well, I was purported to be the greatest cocksman in Miami, and I valued the good opinion of my three friends. If Larry helped me, and I knew how eagerly he would volunteer if I asked him for help, it would all come out—the entire story—and he, in turn, would tell Don and Eddie . . .

The phone rang, a single ring, and stopped. I waited, counting. A minute later, it rang again. This was my private signal. During daylight hours, from eight to five, I never answered the phone unless I was called in this special way. I didn't want anyone from the company to call me from New Jersey and find me at home, particularly if that was the day I was supposed to be in Palm Beach or Key West. My immediate supervisor, Julie Westphal, the district manager in Atlanta, knew about my special ring, but we were close friends. I was his best detail man in the field, and we always had a good time together when he came to see me in Miami. A few women, perhaps a dozen, had been told about the two rings, and also Larry, Don, and Eddie, of course—but no one else. I picked up the phone.

"Hi," I said.

"Tom Davies." The solemn voice paused, and then Tom laughed.

"Tom, you bastard," I said. "how did you get onto my secret ring?"

"I called Julie, in Atlanta. You know I don't give a shit anyway, Hank, whatever you do, but this is an emergency and I had to get ahold of you. I was afraid you might get away this morning and go to Lauderdale or Palm Beach, and it's important that I see you."

"You mean you want me to fly up to New Jersey, Tom?"

"No." He laughed. "I'm flying down to Miami this afternoon, and I'm going to have a six-hour stopover on my way to San Juan. I'm going to spend a week, maybe ten days, with Gonzales in Puerto Rico. But I want to talk to you, and catch a little sleep at the Airport Hotel before I grab the midnight flight to San Juan . . ."

"Do you want some action, Tom? It's short notice, but I . . ."

"No, but thanks, Hank. I'm really tired—I'll tell you about it when I see you. And I imagine Gonzales has got a few things planned for me anyway in San Juan. So what I'd like you to do is book me a room at the Airport Hotel— I'll be in about five-thirty—and we'll get together for awhile at six, in my room." He lowered his deep voice a full octave. "It's important, Hank. Very important."

"Sure, Tom. No sweat. And if you decide you want some action I can probably take care of that, too. I know a couple of girls in Hialeah who like to play sandwich, and if you say the word, I'll . . ."

"Not this time, Hank. It's business. I haven't slept for twenty-four hours now, and I just want to get a little sack time before midnight, that's all."

"Okay, Tom. I'll see you at the hotel—in the lobby—it's at the end of Concourse Four—at six o'clock."

"Good! We'll have a drink, and talk . . ."

I called the Airport Hotel and made a reservation for Tom Davies.

My throat was dry, and I was a little irritated at Julie for giving out the information about my special ring. But Julie and I were good friends, and it if hadn't been important, very important, Julie sure as hell wouldn't have given the Vice President for Sales this privileged information. Tom Davies, of course, was a damned nice guy, and he had been in the field himself, long before he became a district manager and then a vice president, so he knew what the score was, and how we operated. Perhaps they all knew, the entire executive group in New Jersey, including old Ned Lee, who had founded the company. But we played the game, and we pretended to be working our asses off in the field. And some of us, at least some of the time, actually did work like hell. I certainly had, during my first year, but when your sales are up you can slack off. If they go down, as they will eventually if you quit pushing your product to doctors for several months and they learn about new ones from other companies they want to try, then you've got to get out there and hustle again. All the same, I wondered what it was that was so important that Tom Davies, the Vice President for Sales, would take a layover in Miami to talk to me about in person instead of telling me on the phone.

I hadn't seen Tom Davies in about eight months, not since the last Atlanta meeting, when we had had a hellova good time. We had picked up two showgirl types, big Southern broads six feet tall, and we had stayed over in Atlanta an extra day with these giantesses. When he was working, Tom was a serious man, but he also knew how to unwind when the time came. We had had a lot of fun with those enormous women. But whatever it was Tom wanted to talk to me about, it would have to wait until six P.M.

Right now, I needed to do something about getting a pistol, and my best bet was Alton Thead, J.S.D.

11

My adjustment year in Miami, after getting out of the army, had been a grim and confusing period. I had hated Pittsburgh, a cold and miserable city, and I had made no friends among its residents. I drank and ran around with some of the other officers from the Recruiting Station, and our conversations were usually centered on what we were going to do and where we were going to go after we got out of the service. It had never entered my mind to go home to Michigan. Dearborn, if anything, was a colder and more miserable city than Pittsburgh, and with fewer opportunities.

When a man is finally discharged he is entitled to travel pay to the home of his choice, and when my time came I selected Miami. I had never been here before, but I knew that it was subtropically warm, and I figured that a city of more than one million people was large enough for me to find a place for myself.

I had saved very little money, and I took the first half-way decent job I could find, working as an insurance claims adjuster, which gave me $9,000 a year and the free use of a car. Eight years ago, it was still possible to live on nine thousand a year—if not very well.

I had the G.I. Bill coming, and I considered going to graduate school and working on a Ph.D. My undergraduate degree in Psychology was virtually worthless, but I did not like the field well enough to spend three years torturing rats and doing the other boring things I would have to do to get a terminal degree.

The idea of going to Law School occurred to me after I was assigned to a reserve unit. This small unit, which I was forced to join and remain with for three years after my discharge from active service, was a Military Government Team (Res.). We met at seven-thirty A.M. on Sunday mornings, ostensibly for four hours, but rarely stayed for more than two. The size of the team varied from twelve officers to twenty-five during the three years I served with it. We took turns giving fifty-minute lectures, usually on some political or government subject, as assigned by our commander. He was a lieutenant colonel on Sundays, who worked in a gas station during the week. After pumping gas and changing tires all week, he gloried in his Sunday morning elevation to military power, and made the Army Reserve experience much worse for us than it should have been. We—the other junior Reserve officers—became unified in our hate for this gas pump jockey C.O., and I made a few good friends in the unit. Four or five of the other officers were lawyers, and as I talked with them over coffee after the Sunday morning meetings, I thought that the law might be a way to escape from my deadend job as a claims investigator.

The Law School entrance examination, which I had feared, turned out to be fairly easy, and I passed it with a high score. More than half of the exam was concerned with graphs, charts, and math—which surprised me—but because math and statistics had been my best subjects at

Michigan State, I scored high enough on these sections to make up for the other sections, where my scores were merely average.

I was accepted and I matriculated in the University of Miami night school program. All I had to do was to go to classes for four nights a week for four years, and I would have a J.D.—Juris Doctorate. My first four courses were Torts, Insurance, Reading and Writing for Law, and Introduction to Law, on Monday, Tuesday, Wednesday, and Thursday nights, in that order. Two weeks into the semester, I dropped the first three courses, and I would have dropped Introduction to Law, as well, if it hadn't been for Alton Thead, who taught the course.

Law is dull, but that isn't the only reason I dropped out. In my job as an adjuster, I frequently had to call on people at night, and this conflict made it difficult to attend night classes. My office hours during the day made it impossible for me to find time to study, which meant that I would have had to spend every Saturday, all day, in the Law Library. Sunday mornings were spent at Reserve meetings, and our strict C.O. was a stickler for attendance. If you missed three meetings without obtaining permission to be absent in advance, and he was reluctant about giving permission, too, he would write a letter recommending that you be recalled to active duty for another year. We all lived in fear of this possibiltiy, and he was very anxious to exercise this power.

A seven-day week is not a hardship if a man truly wants to become a lawyer. It is a matter of putting in the four years, of serving the time, and a great many young men stick with it. But to do so requires more than a negative motivation, and my sole motivation for matriculating was that I did not want to be a graduate student in Psychology.

But it was the example of Alton Thead who persuaded me to give up Law School, although he did not set out deliberately to do so. Thead is a fine man, and he has a brilliant mind. He was entertaining, forceful, witty, and fascinating in the classroom, and he relished talking about his own experiences as a practicing lawyer.

Thead had attracted nationwide notoriety in the late 1950's when he found a Jewish male who was willing to sue his parents for circumcising him as a baby. This was the most difficult part, Thead told us in class, finding a young Jew who was willing to go along with this radical suit. Thead's case, of course, was a good one. Circumcision is not necessary medically, except in about four percent of those male children who are circumcised, and Thead had lined up more than two dozen doctors to testify to this fact to the court. Legally, the parents of the young man were in a poor position. They had "tradition" on their side as a precedent, but little else. They had doctors, too, but the best arguments they could muster were those of "sanitation." The fact that a circumcised penis is easier to keep clean than one that is not is a poor excuse for the mutilation of a baby's body and for violating his rights as a human being. Thead's other major argument, which would have been more cogent today, now that the country, as a whole, is more liberally educated sexually, carried little weight with the jury in the '50s. And this clincher (in my opinion, anyway) was that the glans of a circumcised penis becomes tough, and because of the loss of sensitivity, anywhere from twenty to thirty percent of a man's pleasure in sex is lost when the foreskin is removed.

Thead lost the case, which certainly would have had nationwide ramifications if he had won, and he appealed to the Florida Supreme Court. He lost there, too, on a five-four split decision, and then appealed to the U.S. Supreme Court. The U.S. Supreme Court refused to review the case, and that was the end of it. Eventually, I suppose, another lawyer will take it up again, and the mutilation of boy babies in this country will be stopped; but Thead's mistake, which he acknowledged, was in using a Jewish male instead of a WASP. The religious tradition was too much to overcome, all at once, and he should have sued on behalf of a Protestant male instead, avoiding the religious issue altogether.

After losing this case, Thead became involved in an income tax dodge, and almost became disbarred. He advised a Palm Beach client about a tax dodge, and the man was caught later on by the I.R.S. The disgruntled client spread the word that Thead, after advising him, had informed the I.R.S. about the dodge in order to collect the ten percent informer's fee. Several anonymous letters were sent to the Bar Association, but nothing was proved. But once the false rumor got around, Thead had to close his Palm Beach office for lack of business.

He then obtained a private investigator's license in Miami Beach, and lost it through some mysterious technicality—or loophole—discovered by the City Commission. Thead could not tell us the reasons why because the information was still privileged, between Thead and an unnamed client, but he would be able to reveal it some day in his autobiography, he said.

At any rate, Thead had returned to the Harvard Law School and earned a doctorate in Judicial Science, and then obtained a teaching position at the University of Miami Law School.

If the practical practice of law had given such a hard time to a man as brilliant as Thead, I thought, there was little future in it for me. Besides, there are more lawyers per capita in Miami than in any other city of comparable size in the United States—and I intended to make Miami my permanent home. During that single semester, while I took Thead's introductory law course, we became friends.

We were not close friends, but we had a relationship a little deeper than the usual teacher-student friendship because he knew that I was dropping out of Law School at the end of the term.

I hadn't seen Dr. Thead for about three years. Two or three times during the last three years I had driven over to the university to see him, but I hadn't been able to find a place to park. This morning, however, I intended to see him even if I had to park illegally, which I finally had to do. All of the visitor slots were filled, taken in all probability by law students too cheap to buy a five-dollar student decal, so I was forced to park on the grass between a coconut palm and a "No Parking—Anytime" sign.

Eight years ago, when I had gone to law school, very few students wore suits and ties. We had worn, for the most part, shorts and T-shirts, and beards were not uncommon. But the times had changed. I saw a lot of young men with ties, and the only man I saw with a beard was a white-haired old guy who I remembered as having something or other to do with administration in the dean's office. With my relatively short hair and my suit, I probably could have passed as just another, older, student in this new environment. I had called Thead before driving over to the university, and I knew that he was waiting for me.

Thead grinned at me when I entered his cubby-hole office, and stopped writing on his legal pad. He was thinner and smaller than I remembered. I took off my jacket and sat in the single visitor's chair. Wearing a half-smile, Thead looked at me from behind his glasses, and nodded. He took a pack of crumpled short Camels out of his shirt pocket, untangled a boomerang from the cellophane, straightened it, and managed to light it without taking his eyes off mine. This was a neat trick, and I had forgotten how disconcerting it could be.

"You look prosperous, Hank," he said. "How much are you making nowadays?"

"Twenty-two thousand, expenses, and a free Riviera." I shrugged, "And I usually get a Christmas bonus."

"That's two thousand more than I make, and I don't have the use of a free car, so why did you finally decide to visit the old loser?"

"I've tried a few other times, Dr. Thead, but there's no place to park around here. I'm in a 'no parking' area now, and when I asked you for your unlisted home phone, you wouldn't give it to me."

"I finally took the phone out, Hank. An unlisted number doesn't work. Somehow, and there are dozens of ways, students got the number and called me at home. If someone really wants to see me badly enough, he'll find a way, even if he can't find a place to park."

"That's true." I grinned. "A very good friend of mine has a problem, and asked me to help him out. I said I would if I could, and that's why I came to you."

He grinned. "Good. I was afraid that you had gotten into some trouble."

"No, sir. It's a friend. A man has threatened his life, and even took a pot shot at him, and he doesn't know what to do about it."

"The shot missed, I take it?"

"Yes, but it was quite close. Should he ask for police protection?"

"He could, but he wouldn't get it. What did he do—screw the other man's wife?"

"No, but the man thinks he did."

"What makes him think so?"

"The situation he was in made it look bad, that's all. But there's no doubt that the husband is serious. He really intends to shoot my friend."

93

"In that case," Thead said, "your friend had better shoot him first. If he pleads self-defense, he won't get more than two or three years."

"How about a license to carry a gun?"

"It takes a little time. How much time does your friend have?"

"Not much."

"To get a license, it's necessary to write the chief of police a letter and request one. The reason the weapon is needed must also be stated, and it has to be a good one, like carrying large sums of money. In your case, it would be simple. As a detail man, you carry drug samples in your car, and you need to protect them from burglary, right?"

"All my friend carries is credit cards, Dr. Thead. Very little cash."

"How many credit cards?"

"American Express, Diner's, Master Card, and three or four gas cards, I guess."

"There you are, then. Stolen credit cards are worth fifty or sixty bucks apiece on the black market. So there's two-fifty or three hundred bucks already. That's a large sum of money, Hank, even in Miami. The next step is going to the police range. To get a license to carry a weapon, a man has to qualify on the range with his own pistol. The initial fee, if he qualifies on the range and his application is approved by the chief, is seventy-five bucks, plus a twenty-five dollar annual fee after that. So the initial outlay is some spare time, and a hundred dollars. The license is good for Dade County only. If he wants to take the pistol into other counties he has to get another separate license from each county."

"What about carrying a pistol without a license?"

"A man's permitted to carry a pistol in his car, as long as it isn't hidden. He can put it on the seat beside him in

94

plain view. If he keeps it in the glove compartment, the compartment must be locked at all times. They have to let a man carry a gun in his car, Hank. Otherwise, he wouldn't be able to drive home with it from the gun shop, you see."

"So there's no problem in buying a gun?"

"None at all, if you've got the price."

"Thanks, Dr. Thead. I'll tell my friend."

"I'll bet you will. And because he's your friend, Hank, there's no fee for this valuable information."

"He can afford a fee, Dr. Thead. Send me the bill, and I'll see that he sends you the money."

"No fee, Hank. I'd hate to pay the tax on it. When are we going to have lunch?"

"I'll have to call you. My boss is flying in tonight, and I've got a lot of things to do today, but I'll call you soon."

"Please do, Hank. You've put on a few pounds, haven't you?"

"A few, but I still do my fifty push-ups every morning, and I'm on a diet again. I can take off ten pounds in a week. The next time you see me, I'll be back down."

I got up and put on my jacket. It was cool in his office, and there were several things I wanted to talk about with Thead, but I had taken enough of his time already. Besides, I didn't want to confide in him. It was too embarrassing.

"Hank?"

"Sir?"

"Perhaps you'd better tell me your friend's name?"

"Why?"

He shrugged, and then he grinned. "In case the police find his body, I can tell them what his name was."

I shook my head and smiled. "No use you getting involved, Dr. Thead. If something happens to him, I'll tell them his name."

95

"All right—but call me soon."

Outside in the hot sun again, I felt as if I were walking under water as I crossed the courtyard toward the narrow strip of lawn where I had parked my Riviera. Except for two Cuban refugees, looking for goodies in a Dempsey Dumpster, there were no suspicious looking people around. I lit a cigarette, and climbed into my car.

12

The explosion, when I turned on the ignition, was instantaneous, but the engine caught. My foot jammed down involuntarily on the gas pedal, and the engine roared. The engine fan, turning at high speed, forced thin wings of black smoke from under the hood on both sides of the car. For a moment, there had been a high shrill whistle before the explosion. I was startled, and my mind was benumbed by the sudden, unexpected noise. Conscious now of the racing engine, I turned off the ignition, unfastened my seat belt and climbed stiffly out of the car.

I wasn't hurt, and, looking at the hood, I couldn't see any damage to the car. There was only a faint remnant of smoke wisping out from under the closed hood. I was joined by a half-dozen curious students. One of them, a black man, grinned.

"Looks like somebody pulled a trick on you," he said.

"Did any of you guys see anyone around my car?" I said, looking at them. They shuffled back a pace or two. There was some silent head-shaking.

I opened the driver's door, reached under the dash, and

pulled the knob to unlock the hood. There was a scattering of gray flecks of paper littering the engine. A student leaned over to look at the engine, picked up a thin red-and-white wire, and traced it to the battery. The wire was split, and scraped to the copper at the ends, and two thin strands were wound around the terminals. There were some short lengths of the red-and-white wire mixed with the shredded bits of gray paper.

"A Whiz-Bang," the student said. "It can't hurt your car any. It just whistles and makes a loud fire-cracker bang when you turn on the ignition."

I nodded. "But my car was locked. How'd he get inside to open the hood?"

"Maybe you didn't lock the car."

"I always lock it."

"In that case," he said, "he must've unlocked it."

All of the students were grinning now. I grinned, too, trying to make a joke of it. "I'm parked illegally," I said, "so maybe one of your campus cops played the trick on me—as a warning."

One of the students stopped grinning, and frowned. "It isn't really funny, you know," he said. "A man could have a heart attack being shook up like that."

"It scared me, all right," I admitted, dropping the hood and checking to see that it was locked, "but I can take a joke. So if one of you guys did the wiring, there's no hard feelings."

"No one here did it," the black student said. "You can buy those Whiz-Bang devices over at Meadows', but that's not the kind of trick anyone would play on a stranger."

"It was probably someone who knew me, who recognized my car." I shrugged and got into the car again and closed the door.

The students, bored now, drifted away. I turned on the ignition, and switched on the airconditioning. I lit a cigarette, and then stubbed it out. My mouth was too dry to smoke. Then I noticed the small three by five inch card half-hidden beneath the seatbelt on the passenger's side. Printed, in neat block letters, with a ballpoint pen, it read: "IT'S YOU I WANT, LUCKY, NOT AN INNOCENT STUDENT. NEXT TIME YOU WON'T BE SO LUCKY, LUCKY. BETTER SAY YOUR FUCKING PRAYERS."

I put the card into my shirt pocket, swiveled my neck and looked out the back window. The courtyard and the first two-story building of the Law School were behind me. Straight ahead, through the front window, was the vast student union parking lot, with cars as thickly clustered as fruitflies on an overripe mango. Drama students, going toward the Ring Theater, shuffled along in sandals. Others were leaving the student union to attend classes, but I didn't see a middle-aged man wearing a seersucker jacket. Apparently Mr. Wright had followed me and rigged the gag explosive device on my car, but how had he gotten into the car without a key? I was positive that I had locked the car. It's the kind of thing a man does automatically, but being positive wasn't enough. From now on I would have to be absolutely sure.

I left the university, and circled about through the quiet back streets of Coral Gables, checking the rearview mirror to see if I were being followed. These were all placid neighborhood blocks, with very little traffic, and there were no cars behind or in front of me when I finally reached Red Road and turned toward Eighth Street—the Tamiami Trail—or, as the Cubans call it, *Calle Ocho*.

My stomach burned, partly with hunger but mostly with fury—an indignant kind of fury caused by the pointlessness of the trick bomb. A real bomb would have killed me, and I could understand Mr. Wright's reluctance to place a real bomb in the car when he might have inadvertently killed a passing student as I triggered it, but

99

there was still no point in using a firecracker bomb—just to prove that he could have blown me up with a real bomb as easily. He was making a game, or a joke out of my life—or, more logically, he was giving me a second warning, when the shot was warning enough, to make me more alert, or perhaps, a more worthy opponent for him. Perhaps he was trying to make certain that I would try to protect myself against him? Was he giving me a sporting chance because he didn't want to shoot a "sitting duck?"

Whatever his intentions were, I did not intend to let the joke throw me off. I was trying to outguess Mr. Wright, and there was a possibility that he had had a cooling off period, and that he had placed the trick bomb under the hood to show me that he was no longer angry enough to kill me, to carry out his original threat. But if that were true, why would he leave such a threatening note?

I shrugged away these speculations, knowing how useless they were. I knew nothing about Wright the man, the husband, or the killer. To stay alive, I would have to assume—without forgetting it for a second—that Wright meant to kill me, and the best way to prevent him from doing so would be to kill him first.

13

After Twenty-seventh Avenue, driving east, Eighth Street is a one-way, four-laned street. The neighborhoods on both sides, as well as the stores, are almost entirely Spanish-speaking—Cuban, and Puerto Rican, with a scattering of Colombians. There are always two or more people in a car in Little Havana, usually several, and as they—the occupants—drive along, they all talk at once, using both hands, including the driver. Sometimes, a Cuban driver, to make a point to someone in the back seat, will take his hands off the wheel altogether, turn around, and with many gestures, talk animatedly to his passengers in the back while he is still traveling at forty miles per hour. One drives cautiously on Eighth Street, and even more so after it becomes a one-way street. I was looking for the Target Gun Shop, a parking place, and out for other drivers.

I parked on the south side of Eighth, locked my car, and waited for a chance to jaywalk to the other side. The Target Gun Shop had been easy to find. The front of the building was a huge target, with wide, alternating black and white stripes narrowing down to a big circular black bullseye that included the top half of the front door. Running across the street, when my chance came, and heading for that black bullseye door, gave me a queasy feeling.

The store inside, dark and delightfully airconditioned, was much larger than it had appeared from the street. One half of the building was devoted to guns and ammunition, with a half-dozen long glass display cases filled with pistols. There were tables loaded with hunting equipment, holsters, ammo belts, and other war surplus camping equipment. The other half of the building, with a separate entrance inside the store, was an indoor shooting range.

I looked into the display cases at the wide selection of weapons, bewildered by the variety of choices. A middle-aged Cuban, with fluffy gray sideburns, waited on me. His English was excellent, with hardly any accent.

"Look as long as you like," he said, smiling, "and if you want to examine one of the pistols, just tap on the glass and I'll take it out for you."

"I think I'll need some help," I said. "I need a pistol, but they all look about the same to me."

"No, sir. They are not the same. Do you need a weapon for target practice, or merely for protection?"

"Protection?" I looked at him sharply.

He shrugged. "A man must protect his home."

"Yes," I said, "I need a pistol for protection."

"What do you know about guns?"

"Not much, except what I learned in the Army. One thing—when you look at the riflings inside the barrel, it means you've got a muzzle velocity of one hundred yards per second for each complete twist. Eight complete turns in the barrel means eight hundred yards per second."

He laughed, and shook his head. "Not exactly. It would also depend on the bore size, the load, and the barrel length, but these things are not important with small arms. For short range protection, muzzle velocity doesn't

102

mean so much. A nice short-barrelled thirty-eight is a good buy for protection. If you're a very good shot you might perfer a forty-five. But if you are not a marksman, I suggest a thirty-eight, and the ammo's a lot cheaper."

He showed me several .38's and I selected a Police Special with a three-inch barrel. It was a delight to hold in my hand. The price was $180.00, which was more than I had expected to pay for a used pistol, but I handed him my MasterCard.

He filled out the bill of sale and registration papers and asked me to sign them. I slipped the pistol into my hip pocket, and he laughed.

"Hold on, Mr. Norton. I have to have the gun registered. You'll be able to get it in seventy-two hours—three days from now."

"Three days? I need it for protection now."

"That's the time it takes. We do the paperwork for you, you see, but I can't let you take a weapon out that hasn't been registered downtown with Metro. It's the law."

"Okay. Can you rent me a pistol for three days, until mine is registered?"

"That's—just a minute, Mr. Norton. You'd better talk to Mr. Dugan." He went down the counter, and came back with an older, red-haired man who looked as if he had rinsed his face with tomato soup.

"We aren't in the business to rent pistols, Mr. Norton," Mr. Dugan said.

"I understand that, but I carry pharmaceutical supplies in my car, and they need protection until I get the pistol registered."

"Who did you vote for in the last election?"

"That's a personal matter, Mr. Dugan."

"Yes, it is, if you want to keep it personal. Do you mind showing me your voter's registration card?"

103

"Of course not."

The moment he saw my registration card his stiff attitude changed. He smiled, shook my hand, winked, and returned the card. "For a fellow Republican," he said, "we're willing to bend a little, but we have to be careful, you know. Some of these knee-jerk liberals and independents that come in here—well, I don't have to tell you, Mr. Norton." He turned to the Cuban salesman. "Take care of him, José."

I left the Target Gun Shop with a newly-blued, short-barrelled .38; two boxes of ammunition (100 rounds); a soft, plasticene holster, with a chrome clip to hold the holster and gun inside my trousers; a Hoppe's gun cleaning kit; and a free bumper sticker, reading: "WHEN GUNS ARE OUTLAWED, ONLY OUTLAWS WILL HAVE GUNS."

14

When I got back to my apartment I cleaned and oiled the .38 and got used to handling it. I aimed at various things in the living room and squeezed off some dry-run shots, trying to become familiar with the trigger pull. But I was a little afraid of the pistol. The concept of buying a pistol is one thing; to actually buy one and own one and have it in your hand is something else—a step across a dividing line that changes you into a different kind of man. A pistol is often referred to as "the difference," because a man five feet tall with a pistol has made up the difference between himself and an opponent six feet tall. But what I was feeling, as I fooled around with the pistol in my living room, was a psychological difference. I felt a combination of elation and dreadful excitement, together with an eagerness to use the damned pistol—to use it on Mr. Wright.

But I was not a good shot. My Army experience with weapons, as a member of the Adjutant General's Corps, was primarily familiarization firing. During an R.O.T.C. summer camp I had had to qualify with a rifle on the range, but we had only fired five rounds apiece with a .45 on the pistol range, just to give us an idea of what it was like to shoot one.

I boiled four frankfurters and ate them with a bowl of cottage cheese. Every few minutes, I would go to the window, and peek out to check my car. Until this business with Wright was resolved, I would be unable to work. I couldn't park in strange parking lots, nor beside doctors' offices—not if Wright had access to my car. Nor was my car safe on Santana, even though I could look out the window once in awhile to check on it. I couldn't watch it all night—not when I slept.

I had to do something now.

It was now two P.M., and much too early to go to the airport, but I would be safer there if I could lose or elude Wright beforehand. I was too restless and jittery to stay in the apartment.

I loaded the pistol, slipped it into the holster, and left the building. I had debated putting the bumper sticker on my car, but decided against it. If Wright saw the bumper sticker, he might jump to the correct conclusion that I had armed myself, and it seemed to me that I would have a slightly better advantage if he didn't know that I had a weapon.

I had lost Wright, I was certain, when I circled about through the Coral Gables residential sections before going to the gun shop. But the chances were good that he was following me again. To pick me up again all he had to do was to return to my apartment house and wait for me. So although I didn't see him, I made some elaborate maneuvers to lose him in case he was somewhere around.

No one knows Miami any better than I do. I've explored most of Dade County by car. I drove downtown on I-95, left the freeway at Biscayne, and then took the MacArthur Causeway to Miami Beach. I drove up Collins, then came back to Miami via the Venetian Causeway, and picked up I-95 South. Then, by a dangerous maneuver and quite unexpectedly, I cut from the far right lane over to the left lane on a tire-screeching four-lane diagonal cross and made the downtown First Street exit ramp. Anyone following me would have had to know I was going to make this suicidal lane switch to stay with me.

I parked at the Miamarina, had a cup of coffee, and then took the Airport Expressway at a leisurely forty miles per hour to the International Airport. I drove up the departure ramp, turned into the terminal parking building across from the Eastern gate, and parked on the top floor. I locked the .38 in the glove compartment (it is not good to be caught with a loaded pistol in an airport). I locked the Riviera and rode the elevator down to the departing passenger entrance.

It was four-fifteen P.M. I spent the next hour and a half slowly sipping two tall John Collinses at the Airport Lounge, well pleased with myself at the clever way I had lost Mr. Wright, while I waited to see Tom Davies, the Vice President for Sales.

15

The two drinks, together with the illusion of security that I felt at having given Wright the slip, had steadied me, and it was simple to gauge Tom Davies' rôle when I joined him in his hotel room. White linen is back, and Tom was wearing a new white suit, a salmon-colored shirt, and a black-and-gold tie. When he met me at the door and didn't take off his jacket when he invited me to fix myself a drink (Jack Daniels Black, water), I perceived that Tom was playing vice-president.

The last time I had been with Tom, about ten minutes before I had passed out, he had been drunk, giggling helplessly, and the two Amazon showgirls we had picked up in Atlanta had been rubbing his naked body with Johnson's Baby Oil. But during this current meeting in the silent soundproof room in the Airport Hotel, mentioning that particular incident would have been undiplomatic. Taking my cue from Tom, I did not remove my jacket. The drink I mixed was very light indeed—a "social" drink, taken genially by the hard-working star salesman in the field.

Tom was wearing his sincere smile, and his manners were muted. Dale Carnegie. I had taken the Dale Carnegie course, and so had Tom; in fact every man in the company had been forced to take it, and the company, of course, had paid the tab. The problem for two men who have each taken and absorbed the Carnegie techniques is to conceal the fact that they are using them on each other. In this respect, Tom was much better at it than I was because, as a Vice President, with a $70,000 annual salary, plus stock options, he had to be. But I was perceptive enough in this regard, and all I had to do to maintain my deferential employee rôle without appearing to be deferential (the company would not tolerate Uriah Heeps) was to talk and act with Tom as if I, too, were making seventy thousand a year. What I had to be very careful about was to never show that I was superior to Tom in knowledge in any area of discussion, and at the same time, never to reveal abysmal ignorance on any topic discussed. It was quite simple to maintain my rôle with Tom because he made it easy for me, and I admired his skill.

Besides, you can't shit an old shitter.

Tom had been a detail man in the field, and the district manager for Southern California before he had been promoted to Vice President for Sales. He was only thirty-five, goal-oriented, and his chances of succeeding old Ned Lee as president of the company some day were better than those of the other vice presidents I had met in New Jersey.

Tom sat on the edge of the double bed, placed his pale drink on the bedside table, and waved me to the chair by the desk. The chair was more than twelve feet away from the bed, and he was establishing—in case I had failed to notice it already—the distance between us as befitted our rôles. He would begin with an apology, and I waited for it silently, wearing my concerned expression.

110

"I know that six o'clock is an awkward time, Hank, and I'm sorry if you had to break off an engagement of some kind to meet me."

I shook my head. "Not when it's company business, Tom," I said. "Besides, how often do I get a chance to see you?"

I had handled that one neatly, by implying that I had broken an engagement of some kind, and by hinting that I liked him as a person, and not because he was merely a generous boss.

"How well do you know Julie Westphal, Hank?"

"Very well. He's been a friend of mine, and I don't say that just because he's the man who hired me. I like him as my district manager and I think he likes me. Julie was damned helpful to me in the beginning, and I learned a great deal from him."

"He likes you, too, Hank," Tom said, nodding his head approvingly. "In fact, he wanted to come down here from Atlanta with me. Do you know why?"

I shook my head.

Tom laughed. "To help me knock some sense into your head, that's why!"

I smiled. "I'm always receptive to more sense. Any man can use more than he has—so what have I done now?"

"What have you done? I'll tell you what you've done! You've become the best goddamned detail man Lee Labs has got in the field, that's what you've done! And I'm going to tell you something else you don't know. You're the highest paid salesman in the company—or did you suspect it already?"

"No," I said. Then I grinned. "But I was a little puzzled when I only got a five hundred dollar raise this year instead of the usual thousand. What's the matter, Tom? D'you guys think you're paying me too much?"

111

"Frankly, Hank, you weren't supposed to get any raise at all. The only reason you got the five hundred was because I insisted on it. You've had it, Hank. There'll be no more raises. Oh, you'll get your cost of living boosts, of course, and your fair share of the annual bonuses. But your base salary is frozen. As a field detail man, you're now in a dead end job."

"I can get by," I said, shrugging. "In fact, I like my job and living in Miami so well, I'd stay with the company even if you paid me a lot less. In this job, helping doctors, which means, in turn, helping sick people, I fulfill myself every single day. It would be pretty hard for me to find a selling job of any other kind as psychologically satisfying."

Tom nodded. "I wish more of our salesmen felt as you do, Hank." He sighed, and shook his head. "However, a dead end job is a dead end job, and you're thirty-two years old. You were offered the district manager's position in Syracuse, and you turned it down . . ."

"I explained that . . ."

"Let me finish, Hank. Sure you turned it down, and I don't blame you. I wouldn't want to live in Syracuse myself. It takes a peculiar and hardy breed of man to brave those Syracuse winters, holding onto ropes as they walk windy streets full of snow, and I was against the idea of asking a man from Florida to take it in the first place. And I told them so emphatically in the executive session. No one held that against you, Hank.

"But then you turned down Cleveland."

"I know, Tom, but Cleveland—Jesus."

"I agree, Hank. 'Cleveland—Jesus!' " He laughed. "The only way we got Fenwick to take Cleveland was to give him a lifetime pass to all the Browns' football games."

"I didn't know that, Tom. In lieu of the salary raise you're not going to give me, I'll gladly take a lifetime pass to all the Dolphin games."

112

Tom laughed. "Who wouldn't? For a lifetime pass to the Dolphin games, I'd trade jobs with you myself! But seriously, Hank, those offers—Syracuse and Cleveland— were not made lightly. Any and all promotions are considered in depth. Lee Labs is a quality company, and when we promote a man from the field, we're looking ahead to at least one or two promotions beyond that one. Now, have you ever heard the old saying, 'Three's the charm?' "

I nodded.

"Well, that's it. When the third promotion is turned down, although it rarely happens, we never make another offer. That's it, and I want you to understand this, Hank. So listen carefully, and let me give you the pitch." He paused dramatically, stared into my eyes, nodded three times, and said, "Chicago."

"Chicago? I think I told you once before, Tom—in fact I'm sure I did—that I planned on staying in Miami for the rest of my life. I'm putting down roots here, I love the climate, I . . ."

"Hold on, Hank. Do you think I'm a fool? Listen to me." He rose, walked toward me, and stopped three feet away. Now I had to look up at him to make eye contact.

"When I said Chicago, I didn't mean that you'd be the Chicago *salesman,* for Christ's sake! We've already got two detail men in Chicago. I'm offering you the midwestern *district!* If you told me you liked Chicago, or wanted to live there, I'd think you had rocks in your head. But you'll only be in Chicago on weekends as the district manager. Your headquarters'll be there—no office—you'll work out of your apartment and get your mail there, but during the week you'll be on the road. Let me lay it out, and if you want to turn it down after I tell you about it, that's your decision. Okay? On Sunday night, you leave O'Hare International and fly to the Twin Cities. A day in St. Paul,

113

and a day in Minneapolis. Tuesday night you fly to St. Louis, and spend the day there. Wednesday, you're in Iowa City, and maybe, every other week, you can make the hop to Butte on Wednesday instead of hitting Iowa City. Thursday you're in Indianapolis, Friday you're in Detroit, and by Friday night cocktail hour you're back in Chicago. If you want to, once in a while, you can skip Detroit and spend the day checking out your two detail men in Chicago. That'll give you a one-day breather once in a while. The thing is, Hank, the midwest is our weakest district in sales. We've picked good young men with a lot of potential in those cities, but they aren't salesmen—not yet they aren't—but we're counting on you to move their asses, to make hotshots out of 'em."

"I just don't want to leave Miami, Tom. I think I'm doing a good job for the company here . . ."

"Good? You're doing a fantastic job down here! When was the last time Julie Westphal came down from Atlanta to critique your sales pitches?"

"I don't want to get Julie in trouble, Tom, but he hasn't been down here in more than two months."

Tom grinned. He sat on the desk, which made him still higher than me. Looking at the wall, he placed his left hand on my right shoulder.

"I know the score, Hank. And I've read Julie's reports. He doesn't come down here to check on you because I told him to leave you alone, and because, as he admitted, he was wasting his time checking on you. What can he tell you that you don't know already? We know how high the sales are down here, and if you weren't out there hustling they'd drop. Julie's a damned good man, but he's limited, too, and his position as southeast district manager is his terminal job. That information's in confidence, of course."

"Of course."

"So instead of coming down here, Julie spends some extra time in Auburn and Birmingham where he can help two young salesmen who really need his help. But in your case, Hank, we've got some other plans. With quality production, our expansion is slow, but we *are* expanding. I told you on the phone that I hadn't slept for twenty-four hours, and now I'll tell you why. I spent that time with some lawyers in a hotel room in Boston, and we have just bought Franklin Toothbrushes. You've seen them in drugstores, and it was an additional line we needed. You'll have a sample case of toothbrushes within a week." He grinned, and when Tom grinned, his lips disappeared altogether and his mouth became a shallow U. "You'll never have to buy another toothbrush, Hank."

Tom took my glass, and fixed me another weak drink. I lit another cigarette from the butt I was smoking. I knew better than to chain-smoke, but the damned pressure was getting to me.

When he handed me my fresh drink, I rose, walked to the window, and pulled up the venetian blinds. There was no window; the raised blinds revealed a white concrete wall—how else could they soundproof a room with a plane passing overhead every thirty seconds? I dropped the blinds.

"I'm very flattered, Tom," I said. "But to leave Miami, to leave Florida . . ." I shook my head.

"Okay, Hank, I'll talk about money. Sit down on the bed. You'll be more comfortable there."

He sat on the desk again, and now, as I sat on the bed, the twelve feet of distance was back and he was still looking down on me from his desk seat vantage point. "As a single man, I know you have enough to live on, Hank, and you should be saving a few dollars. I did, when I was in the field, and we're pretty generous with our expense accounts. In some cases, too generous, but I won't go into

115

that with you because you've never been an offender. But the midwest district means a five thousand dollar salary jump, and you'll be on the road five days a week. That means expense account money five days out of seven. Think about it. Don't say anything. Just think about it. Within five more years, and if you've done the job in the midwest we think you'll do, and we do, or we wouldn't have picked you for it, you'll be moving up. Lee Labs has some ambitious plans, and one of these days we're going to establish a Vice President for Training. That's still a part of my load now, training, but with expansion, I'm going to have to let go of a few responsibilities. Not now, and not three years from now, but I'd say that within five years, or maybe four, that position will be an absolute necessity. I'm not promising it to you—I never promise a man shit. But I have a hunch that within five years— maybe four—you're going to *demand* it, and if we don't give you a vice presidency or something comparable another company will. Yes, Hank, I'm afraid you're going to have us over the goddamned barrel."

"What happens if I decide to stay in Miami?"

"Speaking for the company, Hank, nothing could make me any happier! We won't be able to find a man half as good as you are to replace you, and as long as you're here this is one territory that Julie and I don't have to worry about. For the company, it would be a great thing. Fine. We could quit worrying about Miami—for about five years, anyway. But you're a *person,* Hank."

Tom jumped down, crossed to the bed, sat beside me, and put his right arm around my shoulders. He dropped his voice a full octave.

"Let me level with you, Hank. I like you, you horny fucking bastard! You know that, don't you?"

I nodded.

"You like me, too, don't you, Hank? Haven't we had a few good times together?"

"You know what I think of you, Tom."

"Right. So let me tell you a story. You've met Johnny Maldon, I know. He was at the last Atlanta meeting, and you've probably talked to him at other conventions, or seen him anyway. Has Julie ever talked to you about Johnny?"

"No," I lied. "Julie doesn't talk about his other salesmen, unless they've come up with a good idea."

"Good. Johnny hasn't come up with a good idea in ten years, but eighteen years ago he was a damned good man. He was never as good as you, but at least he got out and hustled. A while ago, when I told you that you were Lee's highest paid salesman, I didn't tell you all of it. How much did you make when you were first hired?"

"Nine thousand, and a car."

"That's what Johnny still makes now, Hank! Nine thousand a year and a car. He hasn't had a raise in seven years, and he'll never have another. But Johnny is really our highest paid salesman, Hank, because he's really making nine thousand dollars an *hour*—the *one* hour, if it's that much, he works for the company during an entire year."

Tom shook his head and sighed.

"So let's say that you stay in Miami, Hank. For the next four or five years, fine. No problems. None for you, none for the company. But every year, inflation. If Johnny can't live on nine thousand a year in Alabama today, do you think you'll be able to survive in Miami on twenty-two thousand, five years from now? In Miami? You'll be bitter, and you'll be unhappy, and you won't blame yourself—no, you'll blame the company. And once you start blaming the company, you'll slack off. You'll work one day a week instead of three or four, and Miami sales will go down. Old

117

Ned Lee won't be around to save your ass, either. Next year, if he keeps his promise, Ned will give up the presidency and confine himself to handling the gavel at monthly board meetings as Chairman of the Board. You'll be thirty-seven years old, and you'll be out on the street, Hank. It's human nature. And even if you continue to do a good job, and I have a hunch that you won't let any bitterness influence your actual working habits, it won't help you. You aren't that kind of man, Hank. But all the same, the other company executives will wonder about you. And why? Because it's un-American to refuse a promotion, that's why. They'll think—right or wrong—that you haven't got any ambition. And if they think you haven't got any ambition, the next thing they'll think is that no matter how good your sales are in Miami—from Key West to Palm Beach— they should be even better, much better—no matter how hard you're actually working."

"Jesus, Tom," I said, "a lot of men keep one job for life ..."

"Of course they do, Hank. But they aren't exactly ambitious men, are they?"

"But if they're happy men, what the hell?"

"Hank, if you're still only making twenty-two grand a year five years from now, I'll guarantee you that you'll be one unhappy sonofabitch in Miami. Believe me. How about one more drink, and then I've got to run you out of here. I've got to get a few hours sleep before my midnight plane."

"I'll pass on the drink, Tom."

"Okay. Don't make your decision now. Think about it— the decision's yours all the way, and I sure as hell don't want to influence you any. Either way you decide is fine with me. I may be your boss, but I'm a better friend than I am a boss, and I think you know that. So either way, I'll back you. Lee Labs is twice as big as it was ten years ago, but we still believe in the personal not the personnel approach to employee relationships. And if the company ever forgets that employees are *people,* I'm getting out myself and they can stick my seventy thousand dollars up their ass!"

He got to his feet, and so did I. I put the glass down on the desk.

"I'll be at the Coronado Beach in San Juan for the next week, or maybe ten days. Gonzales is the only Catholic in the company, and now he wants to hire a black man for the Leeward islands. What do you think about that, Hank?"

"I didn't know that Gonzales was our only Catholic."

"Ned Lee hates Catholics. I thought you knew that. But we had to have a linguist in the Carribean, and Gonzales speaks Spanish, French, and even Haitian patois. Besides, Gonzales is a native Puerto Rican with a B.S. from Tufts."

"I like Gonzales," I said, "I also think it's a good idea to hire a few black detail men—especially if you keep them in the Carribean."

"I agree with you, Hank. In fact, if you take the midwest district, we're going to ask you to recruit a black detail man for Detroit. The guy we've got in Detroit now is afraid to drive a car into some of the sections of his territory."

I started for the door, and Tom grabbed my left elbow with a thumb and forefinger pincers grip.

"So you've got a week, Hank. Call me collect in Puerto Rico at the Coronado Beach when you've decided what you want to do."

"I can tell you right now, Tom . . ."

"I don't want to know now! I want you to think about it, and call me later."

"Right."

When I got downstairs I had a double shot of brandy in the Dobbs House lounge, and then I left the terminal. Tom had manipulated me with a heavy hand. If he hadn't been so tired, and he had looked exhausted, he would have handled the matter much more subtly instead of beating me over the head. Nevertheless, almost half of everything he said was true. I would still get raises in Miami. If I didn't there were other pharmaceutical companies that would hire me at a much higher salary in another year or so. So if Lee didn't pay me what I was entitled to, I would get it elsewhere. But in seven or eight years—not five—I really would be frozen and unable to quit—like Johnny Maldon in Tuscaloosa. In ten years time, however, I hoped to own some rental property, maybe a small apartment house. All I had to do was save my money, but it is hard to save any money in Miami. I would have to work out a regular saving plan of some kind. And soon.

Thanks to Daylight Savings Time, the sun was still shining at eight P.M. I crossed the heavy traffic to the parking garage, and rode the elevator to the top floor. I unlocked my car, glanced at the back seat, and heard, before I accepted the physical evidence, the ticking of an alarm clock. There were four red-and-white wires wrapped around three sticks of dynamite, and these wires were attached to the alarm clock.

Without slamming the door, I turned and started running down the exit ramp, and I didn't stop running until I reached the ground floor.

120

16

On the ground floor, panting, I leaned with both hands against a concrete post and vomited a thin stream of sour bile. My stomach convulsed a few more times, but by breathing heavily through my mouth, I managed to regain control of my body and check my desire for further flight. My shirt was soaked through, and my seersucker suit jacket was damp beneath the arms. I removed my jacket, and wiped my streaming eyes and face with my shirt sleeve.

I had left my car key, on the ring with all of my other keys, in the car door. Cars raced noisily into the parking garage seeking, but not finding, a space on the first floor before they took the ramp on up to the second or the third or fourth. Because I could ride the elevator, I never wasted my time looking for a space on the bottom floor when I came to the airport. I drove to the top floor immediately, where there were almost always empty spaces. I tried to remember what the makes of the other cars up there were, but I couldn't. I also wondered if Mr. Wright was on the top floor, lurking madly about to exult over the explosion.

But, because of the danger, that seemed unlikely. I also wondered what the time was on the alarm clock attached to the dynamite in my back seat.

I looked at my watch. It was eight-twenty-two. If Wright had a sense of order, he would set the explosion for eight-thirty or nine P.M.—if he had a sense of *order*. A man crazy enough to put dynamite in another man's car was unlikely to have a sense of anything. My mind wasn't functioning too well either, or I wouldn't have taken a chance. But I took the chance, hoping, as I rode the elevator to the top floor that I would encounter Mr. Wright. If I did, I would disarm him, feed him his pistol, and then throw the sonofabitch over the rail from the fourth floor and watch him splatter when he hit the asphalt below.

I approached my car. The door was still hanging open. I retrieved my keys, glanced into the back seat, and noticed that the red paper on one of the sticks of dynamite was loose and flapping. I looked a little closer. The exposed end of the dynamite stick resembled a piece of sawed wood. I folded the driver's seat down over the wheel, and gingerly fingered the tissue paper, unfolding it back a little more. It was merely red tissue paper wrapped loosely around a short length of broomstick. So were the other two "sticks." The wires attached to the alarm clock didn't do anything either. There was no battery, and there were no dynamite caps in the three sticks of wood. The bomb was a fake. I threw the wrapped wooden sticks and the alarm clock on the concrete floor and got into the car.

I opened the glove compartment and discovered that my .38 pistol was missing.

There was no way, that I could figure, for Mr. Wright to know—in advance—that I was coming to the airport, unless, of course, he had a tap on my phone. But even so—and a tap was unlikely—he still couldn't know that I was going to park in this particular garage on the top floor. There are literally hundreds of places to park at the Miami airport, and the constant vehicle traffic is unbelievable. Somehow, though, Wright had followed me, watched me, and planted the fake explosive device after stealing my pistol. How, I wondered, did he happen to have a key that fitted my Riviera? And why plant a phony bomb? Why not a real one?

The man was insane, that was all. He had to be. What he was doing, as nearly as I could determine logically, was playing around with me, telling me, in one curious move after another, that he could kill me any time he wanted to, and there was nothing I could do to prevent it. The evil bastard was enjoying himself, and laughing at my antics.

Somehow, he was able to follow me about the city like a damned ghost, and he was able to get into my car every time I left it. He was probably close by now, watching me, even though I couldn't see him. I shivered. On the off chance (or on-chance) that he might have planted a real bomb under the hood this time instead of a Whiz-Bang, I checked under the hood, looked beneath the car, and rummaged around in the trunk. None of my samples was missing, nor had he ripped open any of the sealed cardboard boxes full of drugs in the trunk.

I sat in the front seat, closed the door, turned on the engine and air-conditioning and smoked a cigarette. I was bone-tired. With two bad scares that day, and what with the additional pressure from Tom Davies, my body was running out of adrenaline.

17

By the time I finished the cigarette, I had a plan. A stupid plan, maybe, but I was going to try it anyway. But first I had to eat something—the hell with my diet—I needed all the strength I could muster.

I pulled into the Pigskin Bar-B-Que on LeJeune, and ordered two pork barbecue sandwiches and a double chocolate milkshake. It was the first milkshake I had had in two years, and I had forgotten how good they were. I felt much better after eating, and although I wasn't too optimistic about succeeding with my hastily conceived plan, the fact that I was going to do something to counter Mr. Wright instead of just waiting to see what would happen next gave me a feeling of well-being.

Now, instead of worrying about his uncanny ability to track me through the crowded city, like some wily, citywise Natty Bumppo, I began to worry about the possibility of losing him.

It was dark when I left the Drive-In. I took the Airport Expressway to Miami Beach, hugging the outside lane all the way without driving any faster than forty miles per hour. I didn't want to lose the bastard; I wanted to find him by making it as easy as I could for him to trail me.

In Miami Beach I cruised slowly down Arthur Godfrey Road, turned in to the side street behind the Double X Adult Theater and parked in the tiny parking lot. The old guy who gave me the parking stub asked me if I was going to the Double X Theater, and when I told him I was he reminded me to have the girl at the box office stamp and validate my stub before I came back for the car.

"Otherwise, buddy," he said grumpily, "it'll cost you a buck an hour to park here. This ain't no regular lot, you know, it's for movie patrons."

"I understand," I said. "I've been here before."

There were two films playing. I had seen both of them with Larry when they played at the Kendall mini-theater a few weeks back. The features were *A Hard Man's Good to Find* and *Coming Attractions,* and they were both one-hour length films. That gave me about two hours to see if my plan would work. I took the tire iron out of the trunk, and wrapped it in the oily pink towel I also kept in the trunk.

I gave the Cuban woman in the box office four dollars for admission. She looked sharply at the folded pink towel, and sniffed disdainfully, but that didn't bother me. She probably had a low opinion of all the patrons of the Double X anyway.

I found a seat, and watched a couple of naked blondes massage each other to rock music on the screen for about ten minutes, while I smoked a cigarette and got used to the darkness. There were about thirty people scattered about in the audience. Most of them were men, but there were two white-haired old ladies sitting together, and a couple of younger women—with their dates or husbands— who giggled a lot.

126

I left my seat and went into the lobby. I didn't see Wright in the audience, but I sensed, nevertheless, that he was somewhere about, or knew that I was in the theater. A man stood at the combination candy-and-porno glass counter. In addition to candy and popcorn, there was a wide selection of porno devices and still photos in the glass case. I waited until the man bought a box of popcorn, a Mounds bar, and a French tickler and went into the auditorium before I bought a package of gum from the girl behind the counter. I chewed two sticks in the empty lobby for a minute or so, and entered the men's room when I was sure that the counter girl was watching me.

The window in the crummy little toilet was about four feet above the wash basin. It was three feet wide, triple-paned, and about eighteen inches high. I climbed up on the wash basin, unlatched the window and let it fall back inside against the wall. Then I unhooked the screen, and pushed it outside. The screen fell, clattering, onto the asphalt pavement of the parking lot. I could look out, but the old attendant was at the other end of the lot and hadn't, apparently, heard the screen fall. The drop from the window to the ground outside was about ten feet, which was a safe enough fall if a man slid his body out belly down from the window, and then dropped with his fingers from the ledge.

I took a sheet of the brown blot-don't-rub paper from the container by the sink, and printed "OUT OF ORDER" on it with my ballpoint pen. I had to go over the block letters several times to make it readable on the brown paper. I stuck the improvised sign on the outside of the door to the toilet with chewing gum, and then locked myself inside the cubicle. There was at least a foot and a half of space below the closed door, and beneath the side panel separating the toilet from the urinal. I stood precariously on the seat and crouched down to hide my upper body.

127

There was a tiny screw-hole in the metal side panel, and I could see through it with one eye. I could watch a man standing at the urinal, and I would also be able to get a quick glimpse of anyone who came in through the door.

It was hot in the john. The smelly latrine, unlike the rest of the smelly theater, was not airconditioned, and the slight exertion of climbing onto the wash basin and opening the window had opened my pores. Straight ahead, there was just enough space at the door hinge for me to see the mottled mirror above the wash basin, but not the basin itself. Crouching there, hot, uncomfortable, sweating, with my legs becoming increasingly cramped by the strained position I was in, I felt like a damned fool.

I clutched the wrapped tire iron in my right hand, and resigned myself to a long wait. I would wait out the full two hours, regardless of the discomfort. Sooner or later, Wright would discover that I was missing from the audience, and he would find out that I had come into the john. Perhaps he knew already. When he came in to check, and noticed that the window was open, I would jump him. Such was my simple plan, but the longer I crouched there the dumber it seemed to me.

A young Latin male of twenty or twenty-one came in, and combed his shaggy locks in the mirror. He ambled over to the urinal and unzipped his fly. He masturbated rapidly into the urinal as I watched him in about twenty seconds—zip, zip, zip. This was something I hadn't expected to witness, nor did I want to see it. My face flushed with embarrassment. I could feel the heat in my cheeks. He went back to the wash basin, combed his hair again and, without washing his hands, left the john.

I felt a fresh surge of anger toward Mr. Wright. Because of him I had become a *voyeur*. The fact that it was inadvertent didn't make me feel any better about the sordid spot that I was in. But what the hell did I expect? That's what most of the patrons came to the Double X Theater for and, in the next two hours, I would probably see another dozen men come in and jack off. This dismal prospect so unnerved me that I almost decided to give up my post and try something else, but then the door opened again.

The man who entered had a slight build, and long blond curly hair down to his shoulders. He wore rose-colored Bermuda shorts, tennis shoes with black support socks, and a heavy black denim CPO shirt with the long tails outside the shorts. His skinny white legs were hairless. He crossed quickly to the sink and climbed up on the wash basin. By raising my head slightly, I could see the back of his head above the door as he peered out the opened window. The long locks fluttered slightly as a gust of humid air came in through the window, and I suspected—and acted on it immediately—that this man might be, could be, Mr. Wright wearing a blonde wig.

I flipped the door lock open and jumped down to the concrete floor simultaneously. My cramped legs tingled painfully as the circulation opened up in them again, but I ignored the pain. As I banged the door open, the man whipped about and jumped down from the sink. The long swing I had already started with the tire iron club caught him a glancing blow on his upper arm before his feet hit the floor. He slipped to his knees, grunted, grabbed his upper left arm with his right hand, and tried to scramble to his feet. My next downward blow, with plenty of leverage on it, caught him squarely between his neck and shoulder. His left arm went limp as it was momentarily paralyzed. He opened his mouth to scream, but I stopped him in time.

"One sound," I said, raising my pink club again, "and you'll be one dead sonofabitch."

His mouth remained open, and as I looked down at him I could see the gold bridgework in his back teeth. He bubbled, but he didn't scream or holler. He whimpered involuntarily, but it was caused by the air being forced out of his throat. This was Mr. Wright, all right, with a blond wig. He would have been recognizable—even if he had shaved his black hairline moustache—if I had suspected a wig. But he had retained the moustache; and his wig, now that I knew he was wearing a wig, made him look obscenely ridiculous. I didn't recall seeing him earlier. The chances are that I had seen him at the airport, or at the university, but hadn't given him a second glance. The disguise was perfect. Middle-aged men with long hair and Bermudas are commonplace, especially on Miami Beach, where this kind of outfit is almost a tourist uniform.

I waited a moment, letting him catch his breath, before I told him to stretch out prone on the floor with his arms in front of him. I lifted his wallet from his left hip pocket, and my .38 pistol from his right hip pocket. His heavy .357 Magnum was in a leather shoulder holster under his left armpit. The loose CPO shirt, with the tails outside the shorts, had concealed it well. When I felt the shouldered gun, I held the muzzle of the .38 at his head, and told him to roll over on his back. With my left hand I awkwardly unbuttoned the shirt, reached in and took the .357 out of the holster. I stuck the heavy weapon into my trousers, and buttoned my jacket in front with my left hand.

I had moved slowly and cautiously during the frisking and without taking my eyes off Wright's face. When a man is crazy, and I was convinced that Wright was crazy, the chance of some unpredictable move is great. Even with both pistols in my possession, and with Wright supine on the floor, with his blond curly wig getting damp from the pool of water and urine below the urinal, I was still afraid of him. Perhaps it was a good thing that I was afraid of him. He witnessed my fear, and he was probably equally fearful that I would do something crazy and unpredictable because I was frightened. But this was no Mexican stand-off. I had the .38 in my hand, and my hatred of this man was so intense I was anxious to squeeze the trigger.

My fury was controlled, however, and I surprised myself with my ability to talk calmly in a natural tone of voice.

"I don't want you to say a word, Mr. Wright. We're going somewhere where we can talk, but until we get there I don't want to hear a sound from you. D'you understand?"

He managed to nod.

"Good. If you had said 'Yes' instead of nodding you wouldn't have got the message. Now you can get up, and put both of your hands into your front pockets. Don't make any quick moves. I've practiced some dry shots with this thirty-eight, and it's got a very light trigger pull."

He got up slowly, and put his hands in his pockets.

"Okay," I said. "Now, when we leave the theater, I'm going to have the woman at the box office validate my parking ticket. So as soon as we leave the front door, you stand with your back to the ticket window and look out at the street. If you want to run, fine. I'll shoot you without thinking about it. But if you want to live, you'll just stand there, waiting until I prod you from behind. Then we're going to the parking lot around to the back, and you'll drive my car as I direct you. D'you understand?"

He bobbed his head, and the damp curls shook.

There was no problem. It was a dark night, and once we rounded the corner and left the streetlights on Arthur Godfrey Road, we left the pedestrians behind as well. I had the .38 in my right jacket pocket, and carried the towel-wrapped bludgeon in my left. Wright walked along slowly about three feet ahead of me. I gave the parking stub to the attendant, and when we got to the car I told Wright to use the key. He had a key all right, and he opened the door and got into the driver's seat. I slammed

131

the door and walked around to the other side. He reached across and unlatched my door so I didn't have to use my key. This kind of cooperation, which was unexpected, only served to increase my wariness of the man.

He wasn't a very good driver, but that was normal. He hadn't driven my car before, and he was listening to my directions at the same time, afraid to make a mistake.

I had remembered the Weinsteins, and their now empty Cresciente condominium apartment.

The Cresciente was on Belle Isle, the first island on the chain of filled islands that made up the Venetian Causeway. Like many of the expensive Miami Beach condos, there was a security man in uniform at the front entrance, and he checked on people who used the visitor's parking slots. The residents, or owners, however, were free to come down the access alley the back way and drive into their own parking spaces beneath the building. Then, by taking the elevator from the parking basement, there was no way for the security man in front to check on their comings and goings. Like everything else in Miami Beach, security is merely another amenity that people pay for without really getting.

The access alley behind the row of apartment houses was barely wide enough for two cars, but there was enough space to park on a narrow back lawn before we got to the Cresciente, and I told Wright to pull onto it. After locking the car, I told Wright to walk ahead of me. We entered the parking garage from the alley, waited for the elevator and took it up to the twelfth floor.

18

There were four apartments on each floor of the Cresciente, so the Weinsteins had to be 12A, B, C, or D. I remembered that Larry had told me the Weinstein apartment was on the Bay side, which meant that it was either B or C. The name on the door to C, which I checked first, was Ralston. I tugged on Wright's arm, and we went down to B. *I. Weinstein.*

"Open the door," I said.

"I don't have a key . . ."

"Open the door."

"What if I can't get it open?"

"Last time. Open the door!"

Wright took out his keys, and opened a slim silver knife attached to the ring (there were a dozen or more keys on the ring), and flicked out a shiny rod so thin it looked like a chromed piece of piano wire. He fiddled with the lock, poking around inside with the rod, and opened the door in about a minute and a half. I reached inside, turned on the light, and gestured for him to precede me. I closed the door, and put on the chain night latch. Then, turning on lamps as we went through the apartment, I pushed him ahead of me into the billiard or snooker room.

Some, but not all, of the furniture had been covered with sheets, mostly pastel colored sheets in pinks and blues. The snooker table was covered with a green, tight-fitting oilcloth cover. I told Wright to climb into one of the high rattan chairs against the wall. I went around to the other side of the table, flipped the switch on the long fluorescent table light above the table, and looked at Wright for a long moment, wondering where to begin.

Sitting there in his poorly fitting Bermudas, and wearing black support socks with his tennis shoes, he certainly didn't look dangerous. In fact, he had given me less trouble than I'd expected. But I felt much safer with the width of the snooker table between us. I knew what a poor shot I was, so I put the .357 Magnum down on the table within easy reach of my left hand. In case he jumped me and I had to start shooting, I figured that I would be able to get at least one of twelve rounds into him.

Behind me, the heavy, dark green velvet drapes were drawn. The room was so silent I could barely hear the hiss of the airconditioners. They were set high, about eighty, as is usual when you leave your apartment for an extended period of time. As soon as the temperature rose above eighty degrees, the thermostat would automatically kick in the condenser until it got back down to eighty. I would have reset it at seventy, but I didn't know where the thermostat was. I took off my jacket instead, and placed it on the table.

"Now that I've got you here, Mr. Wright," I said, "I don't know exactly what I'm going to do with you, but first . . ."

"You're going to kill me," he said calmly.

"No," I said, "I'm not going to kill you, but I've got to do something or other, explain the facts to you, or something, to get you off my fucking back. First of all, I didn't screw Jannaire—your wife."

134

"I think you screwed her all right," he said, "but I don't care about that."

"If you don't care about that, why have you been trying to kill me?"

"I haven't been trying to kill you, Mr. Norton. I've been trying to scare you. If I'd wanted to kill you I could've hit you the first day I came to town, and taken the United breakfast flight back to Jacksonville. I knew it was a mistake, and I told Miss Jannaire so, but she wouldn't listen to me."

"*Miss* Jannaire?"

"That's right. I don't have to tell you nothing. I know you're going to shoot me anyway, but as long's I'm talking and you're listening I'm still sitting here. And sitting and talking is still living."

"Wait a minute. Why'd you call your wife 'Miss Jannaire'?"

"She isn't my wife. She's my employer."

"Start from the beginning. I've been suspecting a set-up, but it looks worse than I thought."

"From the beginning?"

"From the beginning."

"Well, first I got this phone call from my contact here in Miami."

"Who was that?"

"I can't tell you that. It's unethical, but I can tell you the rest if you want."

"I want. Go ahead."

"Well, my contact said he had a contract for me down here, and he gave me Miss Jannaire's phone number to call when I got down here, and my password."

"Password? How come?"

"That way, Miss Jannaire would know it was me, and not some guy trying to sell her dance lessons on the phone or something. So I called her from the airport. I had my bag and everythng, and she told me to take a cab over to her apartment. She put me up in her guest room."

"When was this?"

"Two weeks ago. Almost. Twelve days, counting today."

"What took you so long to come after me?"

"We was dickering. I didn't like the set-up. Then my beeper set got messed up, and I had to drive up to Fort Lauderdale where there was a guy who could fix it. It's good when it works, but when it ain't working, it ain't worth a damn. I paid seven hundred and fifty bucks for it, and I thought at first I was gypped until I learned how to use it. My son and I practiced with it all over Jax, with him driving his car with a head start and me trying to find him until I finally got the hang of it."

"Wait a minute, Mr. Wright. What's the beeper got to do with Jannaire? You're getting off the track."

"Not with the beeper. You see, that's how I followed you. I planted the transmitter in your gas tank, and then with my sonic receiver I could sort of run you down. It takes a little time, and if you don't know how to work it, you might as well quit. But I know how to work it, thanks to my son having the patience to drive all over Jax for about six weeks with me chasing him. Of course, with Francis, it was sort of a game with him. But it was just hard, hot work for me. But I found out I wasn't gypped on the beeper set. I know how to use it now."

"Okay. That's interesting. You could trail me with a sonic beeper. That explains part of the mystery. How'd you get a duplicate key to my car?"

"From this same guy in Lauderdale. It cost me ten bucks. If I'd had more time, if Miss Jannaire had told me the make of your car and all before I come down, I could've sent away for one and got it for five bucks."

"Sent away where?"

"Lots of places. They advertise keys in the car

136

magazines. Don't you ever read the classifieds in the car magazines? You can get a key to any make car and year you want for five bucks. But this guy in Lauderdale, he charged me ten, and I give it to him because of the shortness of time."

"All right. Let's get back to Jannaire. She hired you, somehow, to kill me. Is that right?"

"No. That's what I thought it was when my contact down here called me. He told me he had this contract for me, and a contract means a hit, so that's what I thought. I think she had the same idea when she talked to my contact here, but she changed her mind later."

"Who was the contact?"

"I can't tell you that. It's unethical."

"Maybe it is, but I can't help wondering how she found out how to go about hiring a pro killer, that's all. She's a dress designer who dabbles some in real estate, isn't she?"

"I don't know. I don't care what people do for a living. I've got my living to make, and they got theirs. I offer a service, and if they can pay, they get it."

"How much do you get for killing a man?"

"Two thousand dollars. In advance. I've got more, but I won't work for no less. And I do it clean. I come in, I find the guy, and I hit him. Like that. Then I'm long gone back to Jax."

"Why'd she want you to kill me?"

"She didn't say, and I didn't ask. Besides, she didn't want me to kill you. She wanted me to run you out of town instead. That's what caused a lot more delay, you see. It's one thing to come into town, hit a man—nice and clean—and then get out. But to scare a man so bad he'll just pick up and leave, that's stupid. Maybe, in time, I could've scared you out. I just don't know about that now. But even if I did, you'd come back probably. And there was a lot of danger exposing myself to you that way, pre-

137

tending to be her husband. That's why I couldn't say much to you in her apartment. Just the little we talked, you wondered why a woman like that would marry a man like me, didn't you?"

"Yes. I wondered about that. But I didn't think too much about it because I was surprised to find out that she had a husband in the first place."

"Well, I ain't him, Mr. Norton. She might have one someplace, but I ain't married to her. And I'm glad I'm not, either. I'm a widower. There's just me and my son, Francis, and our little grocery store. And that's what I'd like to go on being: a widower. It was the money, Mr. Norton. I hope you know that I ain't got nothing personal against you. Tell you the truth, I felt sorry for you, all mixed up with that woman, a woman that don't shave under her arms or anything."

"It doesn't reassure me, Wright, to know that you didn't do all these things for personal reasons."

"I know. I just put that in. I know you're going to kill me, but it won't make it easy for you if you get to feeling sorry for me."

"I don't feel sorry for you, Wright. I've never met a professional killer, or a hit-man before, but I don't like you personally, Mr. Wright."

"I'm not a hit man all the time, though. That's the problem. My son and me got us a small neighborhood grocery store, and the big chains've made it tough on us the last few years, what with cut rate prices and all. But the last year or so, what with rising costs, we been breaking even again. For the last year, and I could prove it to you if you want, there is hardly any difference in prices. With just me and Francis running the store, we don't have their big overhead, you see—not with inflation, so . . ."

"I don't care about your damned grocery store. I want

138

to know why Jannaire hired you to kill me, and why she changed her mind, and why she wanted you to run me out of town."

"I don't know. I never hired out to no woman before, so it was different with her. Maybe she got chicken-hearted. Anyway, if I hadn't needed the money, I would've left as soon as she changed her mind. But we got to dickering, and I agreed to do it, with her giving me amateur advice ever step of the way. What I did, you see, was up the price to twenty-five hundred. If you kill a man, that's it. No danger. But fooling around this way, trying funny tricks and all, the man gets to know you, who you are, maybe, and then he comes after you instead of leaving town. Or, he leaves town, and then maybe he hires a man to hit you sometime. It's worth more, so I charged more. But she shaved me down to twenty-two hundred. I needed the money, and I would've gone back to my flat two thousand, but she ain't as good at dickering as she thinks she is."

"I never thought about it, Wright, but in a logical sense, the job was worth more than a flat two thousand. Because I did come after you, and I did get you."

"I told her that might happen. And now you're going to kill me."

"No," I said, "I'm not going to kill you."

But I was, and I had known all along that I was going to kill him, just as he had known all along that I was going to kill him. I certainly didn't intend to kill him at first, and I'm not sure when I passed the point when I knew I was going to kill him, that I was going to *have* to kill him, because I didn't allow myself to think about it. But everything he said was reinforcement. For some minutes now, I had merely been delaying the inevitable. I still needed more delay, and I still didn't want to think about it.

139

"How many men have you hit, Mr. Wright?"

"Twenty-seven. But you're the first man I've ever tried to scare out of town."

"How many has your son killed?"

"None. He don't know nothing about what I do when I go out of town. He thinks I've got some investments that pay off just when we need the money for the store. The store's in his name, and he won't be coming after you, Mr. Norton, so you don't have to worry none about that."

"I was worrying about it, to tell you the truth."

"I know you were, but you don't have to worry none about Francis."

I took out a cigarette, and lit it awkwardly, without putting the pistol down. "Would you like a cigarette, Mr. Wright?"

"Are you going to shoot me now?"

"Of course not. I just asked you if you wanted a cigarette."

"No, I don't smoke much. Sometimes a good cigar, but I don't care for cigarettes. I just thought . . ."

His voice was normal, resigned. He had had a pretty good run—twenty-seven murders, unless he was lying—and he had prepared himself for the same eventual ending. His quiet acceptance of the situation was unnerving, and I tried to close off my mind. I couldn't allow myself to think about it. Otherwise, I wouldn't be able to do it. Except for the patch of vitiligo on his forehead which had turned from pink to almost white, there was no evidence of fear in his face.

"Suppose, Mr. Wright, suppose, now, that I let you go? What would you do?"

"Well," he said, "I took the money from Miss Jannaire, and I mailed it to Francis, you see. He's probably paid a few bills with it, and all. But even if I still had it, I'd have to carry out the contract. That's the ethical thing to do.

140

Once you take a contract, there can't be no mind-changing going on, because then word gets around. And if the word gets around that you welshed on one, they figure you lost your nerve, and they begin to wonder about the old contracts, you see. If you lost your nerve, you might be willing to talk about them."

"What 'they' is this? I don't believe that Wright is your real name, but I don't think you're any member of some crazy Cracker Mafia, either."

"I can't tell you about the 'they,' Mr. Norton. But I'm not Mafia, no, you're right there. I don't know if I'd do next what I'd planned to do next, but I'd still have to scare you into leaving Miami. That was the contract I took, you see."

"What nasty little trick were you planning next?"

"A beating. I was going to have you beaten. Not too bad, but enough to scare you. No broken bones, or not on the face, but a good beating with bike chains. I wasn't going to tell Miss Jannaire about the beating because I know more about these things than she does. And I think a good beating, with some bad bruises and all, would've scared you pretty bad."

"Yes, it would have. But if I let you go, you wouldn't leave Miami yourself and go back to Jacksonville?"

"It wouldn't do any good if I did. My contact here would get another man, and he'd have to make Miss Jannaire's money good. Even if I gave it back to him to give to someone else, it wouldn't help you any—or me neither."

"Suppose I gave you another fee—say three thousand— to hit Jannaire. Could you do that?"

"No. That wouldn't be ethical."

I put the cigarette out in one of the big sand-filled standing ashtrays.

Wright stiffened visibly, but that was the only movement he made. I shot him, and he tumbled forward out of the chair, curling his body slightly as he died silently on the white shag carpet.

19

The things I had to do took me much longer than they should have because I would pause all of a sudden, struck by the enormity of what I had done, and stand for long moments paralyzed in thought, or not thinking, in a state of dazed bewilderment.

Mr. Wright, a fatalist, accustomed to swift and sudden death, had died with dignity, as a right, as a rite long rehearsed in his mind. Or, to paraphrase the old cliche; "Dying well is the best revenge."

When my time came, as it must, there would be Wright's example to die up to, the measurement of a real man.

This murder of Wright, as necessary as it was, and I would always remind myself that it *was* necessary, and not a gratuitous act, had changed me forever. To kill a man, whether it is necessary or not, whether in anger or in cold blood, is the turning point in the life of the American male. It made me finally a member of the lousy, rotten club, a club I hadn't wanted to join, hadn't applied for, but had joined anyway, the way you accept an unsolicited credit card sent to you through the mail and place it in your wallet.

The report of the .38 had been loud, but here I wasn't concerned about whether the neighbors had heard the shot or not. In a $150,000 apartment, the walls are thick enough to deaden the sound of a .38.

The airconditioner condenser kicked in, and I felt a sudden whiff of cool air on my neck as I stood there, waiting, waiting to see whether Mr. Wright would move again. I couldn't see his upper body, but I could watch his white legs and the purplish snaky looking varicose veins climbing out of the tops of his black support socks.

I put the pistol down, staring at Wright's pale, almost feminine, legs, and willed them not to move. I had willed myself to shoot once because I had to, but I don't believe I could have shot him again, or put a round in the back of his head for a *coup de grace*. As I stood there, frozen, waiting, staring, I felt very close to Larry and Eddie. Larry had killed a thief, when he was still a cop, a legitimate shooting for which he was cleared. Eddie, as a fighter pilot, had killed a good many little brown men in Vietnam on strafing and bombing missions.

In every instance, the killing was justified, as I had so easily justified the killing of Mr. Wright. The thought bothered me, and it was difficult to brush aside. A killing can always be justified, or rationalized.

Perhaps I could have found an alternative, another option, but no other way out occurred to me. So I quit thinking about it. I also resolved not to think about it again, or at least to try not to think about it again.

The deed was done, and there would be no point to brood on the matter and come up with an alternative some five years from now, because I had had to do what I had done at the time.

I went through Mr. Wright's wallet. There was a Gulf credit card made out to L.C. Smith, a Florida driver's license, also in the name of L.C. Smith, and fifty-seven

144

dollars in cash. There was no credit card for a rental car, so I assumed that he had driven his own car down to Miami from Jacksonville. If there is anything harder to do than rent a car without a credit card, I don't know what it is. But fifty-seven dollars was a very small sum of money.

I put the money into my wallet, and searched Wright's other pockets. I found a packet of Barclay's traveler's checks, all twenties, totaling $240.00. They were unsigned, neither on the tops nor on the bottoms. I had no idea how a man could get traveler's checks from a bank without signing them first, unless they were stolen, and I didn't know what to do with them. But no one ever asks for I.D. when a traveler's check is cashed, and these unsigned checks could be used anywhere in the world. I decided to keep them. If I cashed them, one at a time, over a lengthy period, they would be impossible to trace to me.

I put Wright's key ring, with its peculiar collection of keys, in my pocket, too. One of those keys would fit Jannaire's duplex door, and I had a few things to talk about with that woman. There was a package of book matches from Wuv's, a folded length of copper wire, a theater ticket stub and a parking stub from the Double X Theater, and a plug of Brown Mule chewing tobacco with one small bite missing.

Other than that, Wright was clean. His other equipment, including the tools he had been using for his scary tricks, were probably locked in his car. His car was undoubtedly in the Double X Theater lot, but it could stay there. It would be just like him to booby-trap his own car.

I removed the green oilcloth cover from the snooker table, wrapped Mr. Wright's body in it, and carried him into the Weinstein's master bedroom. I placed the body on the bed, and turned on the bedside lamp. In another two months or within six weeks or less, the Weinsteins would return. But within three or four days, even if I turned the airconditioning down to fifty degrees, the body would begin to stink. In fact, he smelled bad already. The heavy mattress would prevent the odor from seeping out through the bottom, but I needed something more to put on top of the body. I went through the apartment and gathered up all of the sheets covering the furniture, and spread them, one at a time, over his body. There were blankets in the linen closet, and I spread these, one at a time, over his body until there were more than two dozen thicknesses, counting the sheets, over him. As well as I could, I tucked in the edges all around the bed.

By this time I was perspiring heavily, and I sat in the high pool chair to smoke a calming cigarette.

I then took my handkerchief and ran it over everything I had touched, or remembered touching, and turned the airconditioning thermostat, which I found in the dining room, down to fifty degrees. I collected the two pistols, turned out the lights, and left the apartment. After wiping the outside doorknob, I took the stairway down to the tenth floor, and pushed the button for the elevator.

No one, luckily, was in the parking garage, and I walked up the alley to my Riviera.

20

When I got to Coral Gables, and parked on Santander, two blocks away from Jannaire's duplex, it was ten minutes after one. I was tired and fuzzy-minded, and it took me a full minute to decide to leave the pistols locked in the glove compartment. Coral Gables, together with Hobe Sound and Palm Beach, is one of the best policed cities in Florida, and I didn't want to run the risk of being picked up with a concealed weapon on my person as I walked to Jannaire's house.

There was a light in the upstairs living room window, but that did not mean that she was still awake. It might have been a burglar light, but I had no intention of ringing her bell anyway. I found the correct key on Wright's key-ring on the third try, let myself in, and climbed the stairs. No one was in the living room.

The door to the guest bedroom was slightly ajar. I flipped on the switch. The bed was made, and there was a packed, but open, suitcase on the bed. Wright's suit jacket was draped over the back of a chair. The bed was made

147

in a hasty, rumpled manner, and I assumed that Wright had made it, not Jannaire. I continued down the hall to Jannaire's bedroom. I flipped on the lights and she didn't waken. There was no overhead, or ceiling light, but both bedlamps came on, and so did a standing lamp, with a bamboo shade, beside a black leather lounge chair.

Jannaire, flat on her back, snored gently, almost daintily, but she slept hard. Her two brown fists, close to her head, were clenched tightly, and the muscles in her tanned forearms were tensed. She wore a pale blue nightgown, and was covered to her waist with a sheet and a bright blue blanket. The airconditioning in the apartment was about seventy, if not lower, and I was comfortable in my jacket.

I sat down in the leather chair, and lit a cigarette. The odor in the room was unpleasant, and I needed the smell of cigarette smoke. In addition to Jannaire's unique odor, the air was stale, and there was an overlay hard to define separately, of baby powder, cold cream, wet leather, and the general odor of sleep itself. I had noticed this phenomenon before; a woman smells differently when she's asleep. The first time I had noticed this phenomenon I wondered if the subconscious overcomes the defenses of the sleeping body. Jannaire looked older in her sleep, too, and I wondered why I had ever thought that she was attractive. In her nightgown, with her apple-hard breasts partly uncovered, and all of her inky black underarm hair exposed, she was about as sexy as a squashed toad. Nor did I have to kiss her to determine how bad her breath undoubtedly was, either.

"Hey," I said lightly, from the chair, "wake up, Jannaire. There's a man in your bedroom."

"Wha?" she said, stirring, but without opening her eyes.

"There's a man in your room, Jannaire, and he wants to talk to you."

She opened her eyes and blinked at me. She rubbed her bare arms with her hands, as she stared at me.

"Mr. Wright, your husband," I said, "sent me to pick up his suitcase. His son's sick, and he had to go home, so he asked me to mail him his suitcase, air freight. Incidentally, is Francis your son, or your husband's son by another marriage?"

"What?" She sat up in bed, and shook her head. "What do you want, Hank? I don't know what you're talking about. I took a sleeping pill, and it really knocked me out. What are you doing here?"

"It's foolish to take sleeping pills, especially at your age, Jannaire. They're a damned poor substitute for natural sleep, and eventually they can ruin your health. A cup of warm cocoa . . ."

"I've gotta go pee. Put some coffee on, Hank. Until I'm awake I don't know what you're talking about." She got out of bed, walked primly—with her knees together—to the bathroom and closed the door.

In the kitchen I put on some water to boil for instant coffee, and discovered that I was ravenous. When Jannaire joined me in the kitchen a few minutes later, I had fixed two pieces of toast, and I was scrambling four eggs. She wore a quilted blue robe, and she had combed her hair and put on some pinkish-white lipstick. Her full lips were poked out surlily as she got down cups and mixed instant coffee and boiling water.

"D'you want some eggs? Toast?" I asked her.

"No. All I want is for you to get out of my house," she said. "If my husband happens to walk in . . ."

"Cut the bullshit, Jannaire. Apparently you weren't listening to me when I woke you up."

"How'd you get in?"

"I told you. I came for Mr. Wright's suitcase."

149

I showed her Wright's ring of keys. I took the scrambled eggs and the toast into the dining room, and she followed me with the two cups of coffee. I had to return to the kitchen to find a fork, and when I got back to the dining room she was sitting at the end of the long glass table, facing me, and staring with an expression that managed to convey fear, hatred, and loathing. I talked to her as I ate, and her expression didn't alter.

"Mr. Wright and I had a long talk, Jannaire, so you can forget about the marriage fabrication. He told me that you paid him to run me out of town. Fine, I am now on my way out, and I dropped by to tell you good-bye. Inasmuch as he asked me in such a nice way, I could hardly refuse, could I? But I want some answers from you before I go. First, you could have had me killed, but then you changed your mind. Why?"

She shrugged. "I didn't want your death on my conscience, although that didn't matter much to me at first. And then, after I got to know you, and realized how much Miami meant to you, it was punishment of a sort—a banishment, and that seemed like a fair substitute. In the abstract, Hank, having you killed seemed like a good idea—and it still does—in the abstract. But when the time came, I had some second thoughts. The possibility that I might have become involved, in case Mr. Wright happened to be caught, occurred to me, and your death didn't seem worth going to prison for . . ."

"Okay. You chickened out. But why did you think about killing me, or having me killed, in the first place? I admit that I lusted after your smelly body, but that's no reason to kill a man!"

Jannaire got up, turned on the lamp in the living room beneath the black-and-white blow-up photo, and returned to her seat. She pointed to the picture.

150

"That's my sister."

"I know. You told me."

"But I didn't tell you her name. Her name is—was—Bernice Kaplan."

"So?"

"You don't even remember her name?"

"Should I? I don't remember any girl who looks remotely like that . . ."

"Bernice was twenty-two when she killed herself, and you're the reason she died."

"Bullshit. I don't know any Bernice Kaplan."

"She was a stewardess, and you knew her all right, you sonofabitch!"

"What was her uniform like?"

"Mustard yellow, with red piping. And she wore a little yellow derby with a red satin hatband."

"I remember her."

"I thought you would. Men usually remember the women they knock up. I know that Bernice had some emotional problems. Most girls do nowadays, and she didn't have to kill herself just because she was pregnant. If she had come to me, I could've paid for an abortion. For that matter, she had enough money to pay for one herself. But she wouldn't have killed herself if she hadn't gotten pregnant, and because you were the one who did it, you shouldn't be allowed to get off scot free."

There was a great deal that I could say in self-defense, but I was unable to say anything. I was faced with a dilemma, a moral decision, and there was no way out of it—not a single way that I could prove my innocence.

I had met Bernice Kaplan at a party. She had been in uniform, and she had to leave early to catch her plane. When she started to call for a cab, I had offered to drive her to the airport. It was an excuse to leave a dull party, and I had been talking to Bernice and thought she was

151

rather cute. In their uniforms, stewardesses always look ten times better than they do in their civilian clothes. It was a hilarious and exciting drive to the airport—a drive that was filled with suspense.

As soon as I got onto the Palmetto Expressway, she had taken off her derby, unzipped my fly, and started to go down on me. It was so unexpected I had laughed, of course, and then I began to wonder about the time. To get her to the airport on time I had to maintain a speed of at least fifty-five miles per hour, I estimated, but at that speed I was covering the distance so quickly I wasn't sure that I would be able to have an orgasm by the time we got to the terminal. The other traffic was distracting, too, and on the Palmetto you have to pay close attention to your driving. There are a lot of crazy people on the Palmetto, and that included, I decided, Bernice Kaplan and myself. As it worked out, however, my orgasm and arrival at the terminal coincided. I rezipped my fly in the yellow loading zone in front of Concourse Nine. Bernice had fewer than three minutes to make her flight, so all I could do was give her my card, with a hasty note scrawled on it, and ask her to call me when she got back into town. She took the card and fled. But I never saw her again, and she never called me.

The point is, I couldn't have made her pregnant, but I couldn't tell Jannaire the truth about our brief encounter. To do so would be too cruel.

Besides, Jannaire wouldn't believe me anyway.

"Jannaire," I said, "I didn't impregnate your sister. I only met her once, and that was at a party with a dozen or more people around. I drove her to the airport and dropped her off at the terminal. There was just enough time to get her there, and we didn't stop on the way. That's the truth of it."

152

Jannaire jumped up, and started toward her purse on the couch. It was a leather pouch—a drawstring type bag—and huge. I left my seat hurriedly and managed to beat her to the purse. The thought hit me that there might be a pistol in the leather bag. I opened it, looked inside, and then handed it to her.

Her upper lip curled. "Did you think I had a gun in my bag?"

"Of course not. I was merely getting it for you, that's all."

She sat on the couch, rummaged around in the bag, and took out a wallet. She opened the wallet, removed a card, and handed it to me. It was my business card. On the back I had written: "You're the greatest!—Hank." I shrugged and returned the card to Jannaire.

"You admitted knowing Bernice, Hank," Jannaire said flatly, "and that isn't the kind of message a satyr like you would write to a young woman of twenty-two you only saw once, and on a short ride to the airport at that."

"It wasn't a short ride," I said defensively, "it was at least nine miles."

"I found this card in her purse when they sent me her effects from Atlanta. She didn't leave a suicide note, but she was four—or almost five—months pregnant. It had to be you, Hank. I wasn't sure until I met you and saw how you acted—like some sex starved maniac—and then I knew damned well it was you. If there was any doubt before—which there wasn't—the fact that you've admitted that you knew Bernice cinches it once and for all."

"If you were interested in meeting me all along, why did you date my friend, Larry Dolman?"

"Your name was on his application as a reference. And you both had the same apartment house address. I thought, and I was right, that through meeting Larry I would meet you. And I wanted a natural meeting, to study you, before I made my move."

153

"All right, that worked. I was taken in. I certainly wouldn't suspect a woman who was dating through a dating service of being married."

"I'm not married."

"I know that, too. Mr. Wright told me. That also bothers me. I've been around the city for a long time, but I sure as hell wouldn't know how to go about hiring a professional murderer. How did you go about it?"

Jannaire looked at me with surprise, arching her brows. "I asked my lawyer. How else?"

"And he told you? Just like that?"

"No. He said he would send me someone, and later on—about two weeks later—he sent me Mr. Wright. Why wouldn't he? I pay him a damned good retainer, and if he can't give me the services I need, I can always take my business to another lawyer. Do you know how many lawyers there are in Miami?"

I nodded. "Yes, strangely enough, I do. There are about twenty thousand lawyers in Dade County."

"There you are."

"There *we* are. I'm innocent, and yet, nothing I've said has made you change your mind about me—has it?"

"No. I know, we both know, that you're the indirect cause of my sister's suicide. And I think I'm letting you off lightly by banishing you from Miami instead of having you killed. Besides, it's better this way. If you didn't know why you were killed, it wouldn't have been enough punishment. This way, every time you think about Miami—wherever you are or happen to be—you'll be forced to think about that poor kid and what you did to her!"

Jannaire started to cry, and it made her angry because she cried in front of me. She tried to stop, but she couldn't, even though she kept throwing her head back and shaking it, and wiping the tears from her cheeks with the backs of her hands.

"I'll get Mr. Wright's suitcase and go," I said. "I promised to mail it to him."

I went into the guest bedroom, put the suit jacket into the suitcase, and then got Wright's toilet articles from the small guest bathroom. I packed these, and closed the suitcase.

In the living room, before reaching the door, I put the suitcase down and turned toward Jannaire. She had regained control of herself, and she held a crumpled Kleenex in her hand.

"Dark Passage," I said.

"What?"

"Dark Passage. That's the name of that Bogart film where he had the plastic surgery and turned out to be Bogart."

"No." She shook her head. "That wasn't the title."

"Maybe not. But in the movie, Bogey cleared himself, and didn't have to go back to prison."

"You aren't cleared. When are you leaving, Hank?"

"In about three, maybe four, days."

"I'll check, you know."

"Why don't you let your lawyer do it?"

"That's what I intend to do."

I left the apartment without saying good-bye.

I walked back to the car, and put the suitcase in the trunk. I would drop the suitcase into a Goodwill collection box on the way home. Then, after I slept for about four hours, I would call Tom Davies in San Juan and tell him that I would accept the midwest district managership. He would be pleased. I would go to the New Jersey home offices for a one-week briefing—and then—Chicago, cold, freezing, miserable Chicago.

And then I thought again.

I still had the keys to Jannaire's apartment. I still had

two pistols, a .38 and a .357 Magnum. All I had to do was to go back to the apartment, shoot Jannaire between the eyes, and come back to my car and drive home. Who would know? Who would ever suspect me? No one. I could do it easily, and I wouldn't have to call Tom—I could stay in Miami until I died. I could use the borrowed .38 from the Target Gun Shop. When I returned it, and it was back in the glass case, I could tell the salesman I wanted that .38 instead of the one I had purchased. After I bought it, I could throw it away. There was absolutely no way that I could be caught. Humming to myself, I put the .38 in my jacket pocket, and got out of the car . . .

Ha Ha Ha Ha Ha—Ha Ha Ha